He went up the stairs, fighting back the pain that seared his ribs. He ignored the twisted knots that pulsed at his temples. He forced his attention to the decor, admiring the thirties Art Deco.

At the top of the stairs Carver stopped. He forced himself not to stare.

The door to Royal Blue's apartment hung twisted in its frame, hanging by one bent bottom hinge. The frame around the lock was splintered. The door had been kicked open. The dark rooms beyond were a mess, shadowy up-tilted chairs, wall pictures askew. . . .

"Don't . . . don't move," a woman's voice behind him whispered. "I'll kill you. . . . I swear I will. . . ."

Also by Kenn Davis
Published by Fawcett Books:

WORDS CAN KILL
MELTING POINT
AS OCTOBER DIES
NIJINSKY IS DEAD
ACTS OF HOMICIDE

BLOOD OF POETS

Kenn Davis

FAWCETT GOLD MEDAL • NEW YORK

For long gone friends, Richard Brautigan
and Bernie Uranovitzs
who taught us what poetry was, could be,
should be, and is.

BLOOD OF POETS

PROLOGUE

"Relax, lady," the police officer said. "One finger at a time. Just let me do the work. Relax your fingers. The ink will come off pretty easy." He grinned at the woman he was fingerprinting. "We don't want you to get ink stains on any a those pretty poems you write."

The woman, in her early forties, looked blankly at him.

She was attractive, with an olive-skinned Latin quality, her black hair subtly gray. Her eyes had the raven depths of a wishing well built in some enchanted dark forest.

She had said little since being arrested. Perhaps she was in shock? Perhaps disbelief had stunned her into silence?

"*. . . you have the right to remain silent . . .*"

Perhaps the words of the arresting officer who had informed her of her legal rights had forced her to silence.

Or perhaps she was merely waiting for the indifferent ground mills of the gods to proceed at an inexorable pace before demanding her legally allowed telephone call.

She wiped her ink-stained fingers on paper towels. A second police officer led her to a room that had a mug-shot camera. A female officer stood behind the camera.

The woman was told to stand against a wall. The male cop ordered her to hold a numbered slate at her neckline. The female officer at the camera paused as she focused the camera lens on the dark-haired woman. She gestured to the cop who had brought in the suspect.

"You know who she is?" she whispered to the male cop.

"Yeah. Laura something," he said, and then looked at a card in his hand. "Laura De Anza. You know her?"

"Sure," she said. "Don't you recognize her? she's De Anza's wife. Lieutenant De Anza."

"No shit?"

"I'm tellin' you," she said, and clicked the camera shutter.

"De Anza, huh? The homicide detective. I'll be fucked."

"What's she charged with?" she asked.

"Murder," the cop answered.

ONE

A fine mist covered the city from the Pacific Ocean beach to the piers along the embarcadero of the bay. A lone ghost-like freighter circled under the Bay Bridge. The skyline of hills and office buildings was muted, as if pressed against a winding-sheet. The sounds of traffic were stilled.

On Buchanan Street, homicide detective Lieutenant Raphael De Anza pressed the doorbell of a Victorian house. He was tired, and he waited. Most people don't like their doorbells ringing at seven o'clock in the morning. He knew and understood that.

After many years on the job, few aberrations of humanity surprised him. But now—now he felt a cold confusion crushing his heart. Laura. Laura, his beloved wife of eighteen years, was in the worst possible trouble.

De Anza was of medium build, just skimming over the minimum-height requirement for the police department. A thick bandit's mustache accented his upper lip. A beige raincoat was protection against the drizzly morning. He wore a gray hat, and not just for the weather; Raphael De Anza was a hat man.

He paced between the two pillars that flanked the porch. De Anza read a plaque attached to one pillar:

CONFIDENTIAL
INVESTIGATIONS

The door opened.

"Yes?" A lovely black woman asked. She clutched a frilly robe close to her body. Which made her breasts seem more voluptuous. She rubbed her eyes and squinted at De Anza. "What's the idea anyway?"

He guessed her to be under thirty, but pushing that magic age. Pushing, nudging, what difference did it make? He was beyond thirty by more than a decade.

She seemed familiar to him but concern for his wife turned his thoughts into chaos; he couldn't connect a name with the face. He showed the woman his detective shield.

"I'm a friend of Carver's," De Anza said. "Tell him I'd like to see him."

"I see the gold, but hear no name. Whom, I say whom, shall I say is calling?"

"Lieutenant De Anza."

The door closed, and De Anza rubbed his hands against the chill of the morning mist. He was certain it was going to rain again. He thrust his hands into his raincoat and fingered the slim book in one pocket. Laura's poetry.

He remembered who the black woman was: Claire Overton—a local TV talk show hostess who had a show in the late morning. Then he recalled—several weeks previous Carver had been interviewed on Overton's show. *Sí*, that would explain much.

"Morning, Lieutenant," a voice said behind him.

De Anza turned and faced Rose Weinbaum, Carver Bascombe's partner and secretary. Arriving early. He nodded to her, but couldn't bring himself to make polite talk. Rose shrugged and unlocked the front door. She motioned De Anza inside, removed her damp coat, and shook out her umbrella.

The narrow foyer gleamed with polished hardwood. On De Anza's right a staircase went up to the second floor. On

4

the left were sliding doors, which De Anza knew opened to Rose's office.

Pleasant coffee smells drifted down the hall and mingled with the smell of soapy hot water. The kitchen was at the rear of the hallway, and the bedrooms and bathrooms were upstairs. One smell drifted up, the other oozed down, coffee and soap.

"I didn't know," De Anza said, "that Carver and Overton were—how long have they been . . . ?"

"Too long," she said.

"Rose—do I detect a note of antagonism?"

"You're a good detective, Raphael," she said. "But it's Carver's business—not mine."

Rose Weinbaum was a thin, plain-looking woman, with hair the color of a muddy road. Lately she had taken to wearing more colorful clothing, but the chic look only emphasized her unsophisticated, artless appearance. But her voice—

Rose's voice was sultry, inviting, sexual. To some male telephone callers it might bring visions of a redhead or blonde, with cheesecake calendar curves and wet succulent lips. Her silky voice might suggest a liaison in some discreet out-of-the-way rendezvous.

So much for visions.

De Anza heard Claire Overton on the stairs. She stopped partway and looked at him and Rose. He couldn't help but notice the naked line of leg that showed through a slit in Claire's robe.

"Carver says come in," the young woman said, "and make yourself comfortable. He's in the shower, but he'll be right down."

"Thanks, Miss Overton," De Anza said.

"You know me?"

"Me and about a half million television viewers."

She smiled and went back upstairs. Rose opened the sliding doors and De Anza removed his raincoat and hat.

"Raphael," Rose said, "you didn't come here this early for Coffee Royale and a croissant—anything you want to talk about?"

He shook his head, no. Rose was experienced enough not to prod. She offered him coffee.

5

"Thanks, yes, Rose," he said.

She went down the hall toward the kitchen.

He spent a few minutes admiring the polished woodwork, the prints on the walls. A library shelf of books attracted his attention. He was a Louis L'Amour fan, but he had the habit of looking at what people read; it was a clue—a minor clue—to their character.

A few shelves were filled with law books, brochures on current surveillance devices, electronic wiretapping and recording gadgets. There were also many volumes on art, opera, and literature. Part of one shelf contained works by poets such as Robert Frost, Whitman, Shelley, for the classics, and contemporary verse by Frost, Sandburg, Lamantia, and others.

On one middle shelf were slim volumes by black poets. De Anza was unfamiliar with most of the names—Mari Evans, Don L. Lee, Countee Cullen—but he recognized Langston Hughes and Richard Wright.

He picked out an old dog-eared anthology, *Black Fire*, and began to skim several pages. Bitter stuff.

. . . *sable warriors* . . .

. . . *Niggas on the Lower Eastside* . . .

Yes, bitter angry stuff.

The door slid open and Carver Bascombe stepped in. He trailed wet footprints. One lean brown hand was thrust into the deep pocket of a dark wine-red bathrobe. The thick fabric glistened like silk.

Without a word Carver motioned for his friend to follow him. De Anza replaced the book.

Beyond Carver's old battered desk (brought from his previous Fillmore Street office) was a hand-carved, turn-of-the-century wet bar.

Raphael De Anza was more conscious of the difference in their heights than in the racial difference. De Anza was a good five inches shorter than Carver.

Carver hummed a bit of Mozart and fingered several compact discs cluttered in front of a CD player. De Anza prayed his friend wasn't going to put on any classical music. Beethoven at seven-fifteen wouldn't cut it.

6

Carver selected a disc.

"Don't," De Anza said. "Please."

"Wynton Marsalis?" Carver said. "Trumpet?"

"No."

Carver Bascombe shrugged. Rose returned with three cups and a coffee pot. She set the pot on a sideboard next to the ornate nineteenth-century wet bar.

"What's up, Raf?" Carver asked.

Rose handed out the filled cups and stood nearby, warming her fingers around a heavy mug.

"I didn't know you knew Overton that well," De Anza said and sat on a bar stool and sipped at the coffee.

"Yeah," Carver said. "We sort of hit it off." He looked at the doorway and smiled, as if expecting to see her standing there. "She's a beauty. But—what's bothering you?"

"It's Laura," De Anza said finally. "She was arrested last night for murder."

Carver's eyes flickered and narrowed. He checked the surge of emotion that kicked heavily in his chest. He appeared cool and said nothing. He drank several swallows of coffee.

"A lady poet was murdered last night . . . and they've charged Laura with the killing." De Anza paused. "I want you to work on it, Carver."

"Get her out of jail?"

"No—she's home now. Very distraught as you might imagine—"

"You don't look so good yourself, Raf."

"No, I feel totally out of it. I had to work out a deal with a bail bondsman on a second mortgage." De Anza twisted the fingers of his hands together and stared at the hardwood floor. "She only had to stay in jail a few hours. She says she hated every second of it. But she's holding up okay. Laura's tough; married to me she has to be, I guess."

Carver nodded and they moved to his desk. The homicide detective sat in a chair for clients.

"Laura asked me to hire you," De Anza said. "She trusts you . . . I trust you. She wants someone on her side. We want you to find anyone who saw Laura at the time of the

7

murder—someone who saw her in the rain, walking around, waiting in a doorway. If someone saw Laura twenty blocks away when the murder happened, then obviously she couldn't be in two places at the same time. Please, Carver, *compadre*, find that someone! Then the homicide team will be forced to uncover the real killer.''

"Lieutenant," Rose said, "you know we'll do our best. If anyone can find that alibi, Carver can.''

"I know it's a tall order, one in a thousand—''

"Doesn't Laura trust your own investigating team?'' Carver asked.

Lieutenant Raphael De Anza paused for a long time.

"No, amigo . . . I guess not. They've made their investigation. As far as they're concerned, they've got the best suspect now. Most of the detectives have made up their minds that she's guilty.''

"It figures," Carver said. "Why should they believe her? Just because she's a detective's wife?''

"No, and I'm not assigned to this case. Conflict of interest, too involved, all that *mierda*. And that's okay with me. I find the bastard who framed Laura and I'd kill him.''

Carver nodded. But he knew better. De Anza was a fairer man than that. He brooded and unconsciously rubbed his bare feet together.

"Who's in charge?" Rose asked. "Of the case, I mean.''

"My old partner—Ernie Ludlow. How do you like that?''

"Yeah, he would be," Carver said. Fate likes its jokes, he thought.

"He's teamed with Dan Gulden," De Anza said.

"Does Ludlow believe Laura's innocent?''

"I don't know," De Anza said. "I haven't talked to him or Gulden yet. It's only been a few hours.'' He paused. "Carver, you're one of the best hunters I've ever met. If anyone can find someone who saw my wife, you can.''

Carver thought about Laura and Raphael. Good friends. Years ago De Anza had put up with a lot from a young smart-ass PI who still needed taking down a peg or two. Yeah, a good friend, Raf. A good woman, Laura.

He owed them much. Yeah, he'd find Laura's alibi.

Carver reached into a drawer and pulled out a small recorder. He spoke the date and briefly described the circumstances of De Anza's visit.

"Amigo, you know we'll pay you what we can."

"Raf, you've done plenty for me. Don't worry about the money. I'll find the alibi."

"Damn it, Boss," Rose said shaking her head, "listen to yourself. 'Don't worry about the money'? All we have deposited in our account are checks from Randall's Tan-ta-Mount computers and Trevillion Enterprises. Damn it, at this rate you'll never pay off the bank note on your car. The bank will keep that Jaguar up on blocks forever."

"Forget it, Rose. It'll be fair."

De Anza breathed with relief.

"Raf, what's the back story?" Carver asked.

"You know—Laura began writing poety some years ago—well, she sent the poems out—to big magazines and got rejected. Then she mailed them to small literary magazines, and after about fifty rejections she got accepted and published."

"Good for her," Rose Weinbaum said.

"Now," De Anza continued, "these little magazines hardly ever pay—but the prestige can be terrific. A couple of years ago she got invited into an anthology of American poetry and she joined a local group of poets. They meet at Hatt's Restaurant in North Beach where they have spaghetti and red wine and rave and argue about poetry. Laura loved it. And she liked being taken seriously as a poet."

"More coffee?" Rose asked.

"Muy bien," De Anza said. As Rose refilled the cups, De Anza dug a slim book out of his raincoat and handed it to Carver. "Here's an edition Laura and I had printed up privately. Only a hundred copies. She wanted you to have a copy. She signed it."

"What do you think of her poetry?"

"It's okay," De Anza replied. "Obscure stuff, but very rhythmic, very dark and brooding stuff. It's hard to believe that my Laura could have such stuff in her head."

"Probably recessive genes."

9

"Don't give me that. We both hate sangria and candy skeletons and we don't have a piñata for Christmas."

"Think of what you're missing. Your son won't have any kind of roots."

"You've been reading Alex Haley again," De Anza said. "Anyway, a couple of months ago, the leader of the group— a Japanese/American poet named Harold Yoshima—made a deal in Japan to introduce a lot of American poets to the Japanese reading public. Yoshima and another guy were the editors and they were going to pick the poems. Naturally all the members of the group figured they'd be in the book."

Carver said nothing; he listened.

"The poets were actually going to get paid—and if the Japanese edition sold well, there was a good chance an American publisher would publish it in the U.S."

"I get the picture."

"Well, Yoshima and his partner, a black poet named Jack Bovee, did not pick all of the group members to be published. Needless to say it brought out a lot of bitter feelings." De Anza's voice dropped and he wrung his hands. "There was a lot of hostility, a lot of jealousy. Laura told me about it at the time—"

"Was Laura's poetry selected?"

"Yes, as a matter of fact. And since she's considered a novice, this didn't go down well. I understand a couple of the older poets have big reputations—including the murdered woman, Geraldine Hare. There were arguments, backbiting, and some of their meetings broke out into fights. Laura often tried to mediate, but was told to shut up and butt out. Probably said more poetically, but it amounted to the same thing."

"And last night was big trouble," Carver said.

"You're right. According to Laura—of the twelve members of the poetry group, only seven were there last night—"

"And those were—?"

"Let's see," De Anza said, "Laura said there were the two men, Yoshima and Jack Bovee—and Lorna Stokes, Royal Blue, and Geraldine Hare and Holliday Kraft. Laura made the seventh."

Carver was familiar with some of the names. Royal Blue

was a young black poetess who had earned a bit of notoriety with a five-page poem about orgasms. Lorna Stokes was often called the working woman's poet.

He went to the bookshelves. He searched the index of a current, local, biographic literary journal and found Geraldine Hare's name.

According to the brief biography, Geraldine Hare's poetry was considered up-to-date, although she wrote in a classic style. She selected the patterns of raw life to analyze, and hewed them in meter, rhyme, and rhythm. In the group Hare was probably closest to being a popular poet, moderately well-known even among those who never read poetry.

Carver made a mental note that at a later time he'd study the other poets' works. He brought the books to his desk and asked De Anza to continue.

"Laura often told me that Geraldine Hare had an immense ego. And an anger to match. Last night Hare was particularly vicious. She got into a fight with Lorna Stokes and Laura tried to mediate. . . . Hare screamed at Laura—and there were plenty of witnesses at Hatt's—and attacked her. Laura was shoved onto another patron's table, dumping minestrone all over the place. A lot of the people thought that was pretty damned funny and they laughed. Laura was outraged and told Hare she was going to kill her. A couple of waiters kept them apart. Laura says she went for a long walk to cool off."

"In the rain," Carver said, as he arranged the volumes of verse into a neat stack.

"It wasn't raining at first. She says she walked for about twenty minutes and then the rain started pouring. She ducked into a doorway, but she isn't sure where it was—just somewhere around Nob Hill. She waited it out. Then she walked back to her car and drove home. I wasn't in—"

"So Laura has no alibi—because the cops figured Geraldine Hare was killed during the time of the rain."

"That's almost it. Hare was found in a parking lot of a fast-food place near Columbus Avenue and Fisherman's Wharf. She'd been stabbed. She was facedown—the ground beneath her was dry, but her back was wet. It figures she was killed just before the rain started, and Laura can't prove where she was. That was enough for the arresting officers."

Carver figured the distance between Nob Hill and the fast-food parking lot. About twenty blocks.

Deep down inside Carver an instinct awakened. It was like a hunting beast opening its eyes from hibernation. The feeling was familiar. The ferret-like animal flexed its claws.

"I'll have to talk with Laura," Carver said.

"Amigo, lay off her. You don't need to disturb her. She's been through enough in the past few hours. I'll give you all the information you'll need."

"I must see her, Raf. Otherwise it's just hearsay."

"No," De Anza said. The word jumped out like a sour note in an orchestra. He clenched his fists at his sides.

"Hearsay, Raf. Hearsay. And you know it. I have to ask her about the streets she walked, what she wore, who might have seen her, all that. I'll need to take photos of her to show around."

"No." De Anza glowered, his lips bloodless. "I mean it."

"Laura will be my client. Not you. She has to tell me I'm working for her. This is too important to do it any other way."

"No, absolutely no. She's upset. No!"

"They probably can't afford us," Rose said, getting into the game. She sipped nonchalantly at her coffee.

"That's academic," Carver said.

"All right!" De Anza exploded. "All right! You can see Laura, but God help you if she gets depressed or hysterical. . . ."

"Lieutenant," Rose said, "Laura is tougher than that. This will establish a working relationship between you, Laura, and Carver. You know what the boss does and how he does it. The best."

"He's got to find someone who saw her! I can't have my Laura stand trial!"

"Let's get back to the bucks," Rose parried.

"I'll charge what they can afford," Carver said. "Raphael is a friend."

"Friends don't have money? They don't pay their bills, don't pay their hired help? What are we, on minimum wage like fast-food teenage employees? With clues and witnesses for sale, but only if they cost a couple of bucks an hour?"

Carver and De Anza laughed.

"Don't patronize me," Rose said as she went to her desk and pulled off the typewriter cover. "If we don't get paid, how am I ever going to get a computer word processor and join the capital M, capital P, March of Progress?"

Carver held up a hand for attention. He cocked his ears to the side door that connected his office to the hallway. He *hmmed*, and held a finger to his lips. He motioned for Rose and De Anza to continue speaking. Silently, on bare feet, he moved to the door. He jerked the door open. Claire Overton gasped and jerked back.

"Not smart, Claire," Carver said, his voice hard and crisp.

"I was just passing by—" Claire said, recovering her composure nicely. "I was going to the kitchen to start something for breakfast."

"Sure," Carver said. He paused. "I'll talk to you later."

"Sure," Claire Overton echoed and went down the hall toward the kitchen.

Carver resisted the urge to slam the door; he forced himself to close it gently. At his desk he glared at the scarred wooden top. God, he hated eavesdroppers in his own home. He strained to appear relaxed.

"Right," Carver said to De Anza, "I'll talk with Laura. I promise you that I'll find someone who saw her last night."

"Carver, *compadre*, I'm grateful. If anyone can find her alibi, you can."

Carver nodded. Lieutenant De Anza said good-bye to Rose, took his coat and hat, and left the office.

"Your guest is in deep trouble," Rose said. "Get rid of her, Carver. Claire's not your type." She held up her hands in mock fear. "All right, okay, Boss, I know—it's none of my business. But don't forget—"

"I know, Rose. You own half this house."

Carver Bascombe and Rose Weinbaum had pooled their money and invested in the Victorian on Buchanan Street.

Carver lived in the house and maintained his offices there. Rose was also one-third partner in the private investigation and security company.

Carver held back a smile. Rose. What a woman. Her late husband, Bernie Weinbaum, had trained her well. Rose was one of the best things in Carver's life. She had an instinct for investigative work—probably better than Bernie ever had.

"What's your first step, Carver?" she asked.

"Look around Nob Hill—I'll need a couple of private investigators to help search for Laura's alibi. Then I'll talk to the poets that were at Hatt's."

"Why talk to them? You're supposed to find an alibi."

"Because—since Laura didn't kill Hare—then maybe one of the others did. And apparently the homicide cops aren't checking out the other poets. If they won't, I will."

Oh, yeah, plenty to do, he thought. To canvass the Nob Hill neighborhood where Laura walked would require more manpower.

He thought about which PI's might help: Mike Tettsui? Definitely. Marko Wright? Yeah, a guy who could read people like they were made of clear acrylic. (But couldn't see himself at all.) Olly Demain? No. Good for research, though. (But not as good as Rose Weinbaum.) Bea Murphy? Probably. Another good hunter. A good woman, been around the cage plenty.

Carver wrote down the three likely names:

Mike Tettsui—Marko Wright—Bea Murphy—

He asked Rose to call the three PI'S. Be sure they were available in a few hours.

The office door opened and Claire Overton stepped in. She carried a plate of scrambled eggs and a croissant to the wet bar. Carver swiveled and watched her.

Beautiful. No doubt about that, he thought. Look at those legs; he never tired of looking at those long legs. And her curves were inviting, even hidden somewhat by the dressing gown—full, sensual breasts, and smooth hips, with just a bit of a mound at the pelvis—and a lovely rear.

Claire knew she was lovely, but it ended there. Her desires for fame and glory were the props of her ambition. Carver knew she schemed constantly. Her ambition was immense and she would track down any story as mulch for her morning talk show. Just as she had eavesdropped on Carver's conversation with De Anza. Anything to further her career as a talk show hostess.

He thought, that's what comes from getting interviewed on TV. Meet the hostess, get infatuated, date her, take her to a symphony, take her to bed. That should have been enough, but it wasn't. Claire had a case of terminal curiosity.

She poured a large portion of brandy into a goblet. She tossed off several large swallows and bit off a piece of croissant. She glared at Carver.

"Well?" she said, daring him to say anything.

Carver shrugged.

"Join me," Claire Overton demanded, and her tone meant she didn't include Rose Weinbaum.

At the bar Carver shoved the cork back into the brandy bottle. He told her she'd had enough.

"Jesus H. Christ, are you going to lecture me?" Claire said and drained off the last of the brandy in the goblet. She narrowed her eyes at the bottle. "Don't lecture me, lover. I'm old enough to do what I want. If I want to drink in the morning, I will just goddamn do that."

Carver said nothing. He opened one of the poetry books. Several lines by Geraldine Hare caught his eye—

> *Fear is a fragile glass soon shattered*
> *The splinters reflect life all battered—*

"Okay," Claire said, interrupting his thoughts. The single drawn-out word was burdened with exasperation. "So I overheard you and your cop friend. Homicide detectives don't fall over me every day. You gotta admit he'd make a good subject for my show."

She often talked as though the morning talk show were hers alone, although a popular male co-host was on camera with her.

"Why not?" she continued. "De Anza, right? With his wife charged with murder, I'd say he needed all the sympathetic publicity he can get. And my show reaches almost a million people every morning. I'd say that could only help."

Carver shook his head. Rose entered and walked over to the wet bar. She leaned her elbows on the counter and gazed unblinkingly at Claire.

"I think," Rose said, "it was a mistake for Carver to go on your show. And he knows I think so."

"Easy, Rose," Carver said.

"No, Boss," she replied and looked again at Claire. "She knows how I feel."

"Yes, I know," Claire answered sullenly. She took the brandy bottle and poured herself another goblet full. "I really want to hear what strong and silent has to say about this." She turned her luminous brown eyes on Carver. "What do you say, lover? Does all this really change things?"

Carver rubbed the cleft in his chin. There was no way he could have her stay in the house while he investigated Laura's case. God, it would be like having the ears and mouth of the public in the house. Vox populi.

After several evenings together he had realized that Claire's scruples were in the hands of whimsy and fate. Which is to say, she had no ethics, no scruples. Truth was just a five-letter word. One four-letter word was her truth. *News.* Which was not something to inform the public, but merely something that the competition didn't have.

Every day that she stayed, a battle would rage inside Claire to decide to talk or not about his case on TV.

"Carver, dear," Claire said, "I know what you're thinking. You're worried about my ambition. I admit it's huge. But I have a solution—see if you don't agree this is good. For both of us. You work here—but the rest of the time you stay at my apartment. You know you like it. Great view of the city, Nob Hill, and the bay, and Alcatraz. Oops. I guess I shouldn't have mentioned that. I know you have bad memories about that— Ooops. Maybe I shouldn't have said that either."

"Maybe," Rose suggested, "it's the brandy."

"Claire, your show's at ten," Carver said without emotion. Dangerously lacking in inflection. "Now would be a good time to get dressed to go."

"I'll go, but just to work, Carver. I think you're letting this skinny old white woman run your life. It's not healthy."

"Easy, Claire," he said, the words brittle and hard.

"It's a sick relationship, you a good-looking guy, and this secretary whatever-she-is—a sexpot voice in an anorexic body— She probably practices that voice at home, with a closet of leather underpants—"

"Shut up," Carver commanded.

"What?" she said, her voice rising.

"Shut up."

Claire Overton heaved the brandy bottle at Carver's head. He ducked, and the bottle smashed into the TV set against the far wall. The tube exploded into shards, and sparks and smoke burst out from the innards.

TWO

Tired feet. Hot feet. Wet Feet.

Carver Bascombe lowered himself into a chair. He flipped the daily paper and a book onto the table. He toyed idly with the book, an anthology of current poety. Specs, the bartender and owner, came over and asked if he wanted something— or was he just cooching out of the rain?

Carver ordered an Anchor Steam beer.

The bar at 12 Adler Place was less than half filled. Good

time for thinking. Carver had pushed the ugly scene with Claire from his mind; he had to concentrate on helping Laura De Anza.

After leaving his office, he had visited Laura and heard her story. He was convinced she was telling the truth.

Carver pulled out a set of photos and studied them. He had photographed Laura that morning. One was a full-figure, Polaroid color shot of her in clothing similar (but not exactly like) what she had worn the night before: maroon skirt, heavy ocher V-necked cable sweater, walking shoes, and a wine-red poncho. No umbrella.

The police were checking Laura's clothing for blood-stains. And they were making a fiber analysis of material found on Geraldine Hare's clothing.

The second photo was a close-up of her face.

He had taken three sets of instant photographs and given one set each to Mike Tettsui and Bea Murphy, the two PI's he had hired. He would've preferred working with Marko Wright, but Wright was in Hollywood working as a technical consultant on a private-eye movie.

Carver had shown the photos to dozens of shopkeepers in the neighborhood where Laura had said she had walked. No one remembered ever seeing her.

Which proved nothing.

Specs brought the beer, and Carver slowly savored his favorite brew. He was waiting for Tettsui and Murphy to report in. He hoped they had had better luck than he.

Now it was time to spread the net farther. Down in some primitive layer of humanity, the stalking animal preened itself and bared its teeth.

If Laura didn't kill Geraldine Hare, then obviously some-one else did. What was the motive? Something personal in Hare's past? Did someone hate her? A relative? A lover? Or was it as De Anza suggested—a jealous rage among her peers?

He interrupted his musings to fend off a couple of guys hustling beers. White guys hustling his blackness, using the usual good guy, all-one-world-we're-all-equal kind of cheerful drunkenness. Carver told them both to blow it out their white asses.

They grinned, figuring he didn't mean it. He didn't. The two drunks wandered off to try their happy-go-lucky drunken con on some other patron. Before long, Carver knew, Specs would toss them out the door into the rainy alley.

Specs' place, officially called the 12 Adler Place Museum and Café, was in a short dead-end alley just off the intersection of Columbus and Broadway. Generations of bohemians, beatniks, hippies, and creative (or would-be creative) people had hung out.

Drunken conversation, earnest conversation, bounced and echoed off the brick walls. Carver idly read one of the numerous signs put up by Specs:

> The management spares no expense to
> provide a regulation-size alleyway
> for the settling of physical contests.

Behind the scarred bar counter was an ancient, blackened, rusty-wheel cheese cutter, and several draft beer pumps. Among the NRA signs, dusty flags, block and tackle, and shark's teeth was a jumble of liquor bottles. The bar was a hangout for the weird, the flakes, the searchers for truth. An art hangout. In the center, the hub, of North Beach.

Carver thought about the scene at Hatt's the previous night: Geraldine Hare had been there, and Royal Blue, Lorna Stokes, Jack Bovee, Harold Yoshima, and Holliday Kraft. And Laura, of course.

He opened the book and used the index and selected the biographical sketches to study. Geraldine Hare, the classicist, he had already read about.

The one with the odd name, Royal Blue, had created a stir in local poetry circles with a poem about orgasms. Blue's infamous and controversial poem was a metaphor for equal rights.

Blue's parents, Tom and D'Arlene Blue, had been hippies and flower children. As had so many of their peers, they named their child in a memorable fashion. Royal Blue—a child of those times.

There was Lorna Stokes—who was considered the doyen of working-class women, with poems about the social injustice and inequality of the labor ethic.

Carver dimly recalled reading in the newspaper-book-review section that Stokes had once been married. Now divorced. According to what Laura had told him, Stokes worked as a pizza-delivery driver for the local North Beach Par-Cheesey franchise shop. Only a few blocks away. He decided he'd talk to her first.

Harold Yoshima—the spiritual leader of the group—specialized in the haiku form. His anthologies of poetry were well-known. He had been married once but was now a widower.

Jack Bovee was a poet of the streets, of the working man and woman, of the radical, the hip, the outlawed, and the disenfranchised. Very perceptive work, usually of feelings, free verse. He was supposed to be quite eccentric, something of an ascetic.

His poetic outbursts were well received in the various colleges and universities where he often lectured.

Laura hadn't known Bovee's address.

Holliday Kraft was a reactionary poet, with a talent for composing pretty poems, almost Victorian, about flowers and meadows and trees and sunsets. Her visions of beauty were often criticized by reviewers for her almost purple poetry. She was one of the few who often preferred the old-fashioned traditions of meter—ta-*Tum* ta-*Tum* ta-*Tum*. Iambic.

She was single, and Laura hadn't known where she lived.

Laura had also given him information about jealousies that raged among the group. She considered Lorna Stokes, Harold Yoshima, and Royal Blue her friends. Interesting ones, at least.

Yoshima probably had all the members' addresses and phone numbers. From Laura's home Carver had telephoned Yoshima, but his call was received by an answering machine. Carver didn't leave a message; he figured on phoning later.

Laura hadn't known Harold Yoshima's daytime work number. She thought he worked in some kind of word-processing business. One of the other poets, Jack Bovee, would know.

Carver wanted several items of information. One—where had each poet been at the time of Hare's death, when the rain started? Second, what were their opinions of Geraldine Hare?

Some would tell him the truth. People seldom did, Carver thought. It came with the job. Sooner or later one of them might slip.

The door opened, rain gusted in, and Bea Murphy entered. First of Carver's team to report. She shucked off her gloves and her plastic raincoat, and pulled up a chair next to Carver. Murphy said she had zip-o. Five hours of walking the streets and nothing.

Bea Murphy was a small woman, with rich dark hair pulled back severely into a ponytail. Carver knew the ponytail hid a slender sheathed stiletto. All of Murphy's dresses and blouses had a sheath sewn into the back. Even her one-and-only evening dress.

Other than that, she was a friendly, cheerful woman, with shiny gray eyes and full lips in a round Irish face. About thirty-five, Carver guessed.

"Sorry, lad," Bea Murphy said. "I think it's a bloody waste of time out there. Nobody saw Laura De Anza. Want me to keep going?"

"We'll see," Carver said.

Specs came over and Murphy wanted something hot.

"Hot chocolate?" he suggested.

"You got to be kidding, lad."

"Hot brandy? Hot mulled wine?"

"Hey, the mulled wine, that sounds terrific. And don't forget the cinnamon stick."

"Never," Specs said and went back to the bar.

"Anything in the paper?" Murphy asked.

Carver flipped open the newspaper to the story about Geraldine Hare's death.

"Knifed," he said. "In the back."

Bea Murphy unconsciously stroked the back of her own neck.

About ten minutes later Mike Tettsui came in, shaking the rain off his coat.

Tettsui was a cheerful man, older than Carver by a couple of years, married, with a daughter. He and his family lived in the Richmond district, which had long since been changing to an Asian neighborhood.

He was medium height, wore casual clothing, and intensely disliked wearing ties. Tettsui made a first-rate detective; he trusted very few people and assumed everyone lied to him. But he had a cheerful side, loaded with irreverent humor. Tettsui was the fastest man with a gun Carver Bascombe had ever seen.

"I think," Tettsui said, sliding into a chair, "we're in for another wet forty days and forty nights."

"Nothing then?" Carver said, referring to the search for Laura's alibi.

"No, Carver."

"But then what can you expect?" Murphy said. "Sure, a dark rainy night. A woman in a dark red poncho, dark hair, and if she was like you said, angry and bloody well pissed off, she was probably walking with her head down, talking to herself. Figuring what she should have said to Hare, something really snappy and clever. Kicking herself for letting her anger get the best of her. Who's going to look at a woman like that?"

"It was very dark last night," Tettsui said, "and I have had no success in finding anyone who might have seen Laura De Anza." He shrugged amiably. "But if you wish, at overtime rates of course, I am sure we will all go back onto the streets and continue our search."

Specs delivered Murphy's mulled wine and took an order of bourbon from Tettsui. Carver ordered another Anchor Steam.

"Searching for Laura's alibi during the day accomplishes nothing," Bea Murphy said, swizzling the cinnamon stick into the steaming red wine. "The murder happened at night, and surely that's the time we should be looking."

"It is rumored," Tettsui said, "that the police are not

22

investigating the whereabouts or motives of the other poets who had been at Hatt's."

"They believe they got their killer," Bea Murphy said. "Just like the cops. Why should they check further?"

Specs interrupted the lull by bringing over the drinks.

Bea Murphy drank her mulled wine. She narrowed her eyes at Carver.

"Is that one of them English trench coats?" she asked.

Carver nodded.

"You should be ashamed of yourself."

"I'm just one of the black-and-tan," Carver said.

"Ah, it's not to joke. Them coats don't come cheap. More than I can afford, I tell you. You still wearing those expensive suits? Those bloody Italian things that cost more than I earn in three weeks?"

"Bea," Tettsui said, "leave the man alone. What he pays for his clothes is not our business."

"Sure, sure. I'm just sort of thinking out loud."

"Drop it, then, Bea," Tettsui said, then added, "How about those Forty-Niners?"

Carver and Murphy laughed. Carver tilted back in his chair and thought. Tettsui and Murphy talked quietly and studied their street maps.

Walking Laura's route, Bea had covered the west side of Mason Street, while Mike Tettsui had checked the east side. Carver had walked the remainder of Nob Hill.

It had to be done. And until it became totally hopeless, it had to continue. And it would be damned expensive.

"Keep after the night persons," Carver said. "Somebody saw Laura. A janitor, a street-cleaning-machine operator, cops—cabbies, all-night convenience store clerks—someone."

"What'll you do?" Murphy asked.

"When do we meet again?" Tettsui asked.

"I'll check the poets that were at Hatt's," Carver answered. "If the cops won't—I will. We'll meet tomorrow. Same time, same place. If you get something important, telephone, or get me on my pager."

They nodded and worked on their drinks.

Carver had decided to visit Hatt's—it was only a few blocks

23

away—and question the waiters. And then interview Lorna Stokes, who worked close by. Then he'd talk to Yoshima and ask him for the addresses of Jack Bovee and Holliday Kraft. After that, he'd speak with Royal Blue, who lived close to Yoshima.

That should be enough for one night.

Carver said good-bye to the two PI's. He picked up the books and shoved them into his pocket. Outside he checked his watch: five o'clock. And getting dark. The rain was a steady drizzle. Carver pulled a knitted watch cap from his trench coat and settled it comfortably on his head.

Hatt's would be filling up with the evening's patrons. As Carver walked in, he thumbed on his shirt-pocket-sized recorder.

Nudged by the acquisition of five-dollar bills, several waiters told their impression of the argument. Their versions coincided with Laura De Anza's story.

Geraldine Hare and Lorna Stokes had started out the evening by not talking to each other. Then Geraldine made some cracks about Stokes's poetic abilities. Stokes ignored the jibes, but the remarks became caustic, with Hare calling Stokes "the pizza pusher." Then the thing escalated, and Laura tried to calm the two women down, but Hare slapped her and shoved Laura onto a diner's table, where she got minestrone and spaghetti all over the back of her dress.

Laura was heard by both waiters to curse violently and then say to Geraldine Hare, "I'll kill you for this."

The two waiters didn't know (or wouldn't tell) the addresses of any of the poets. Carver thanked the waiters and left.

Lorna Stokes was closest—at her job at the Par-Cheesey Pizza company. According to Laura, Stokes delivered pizzas in a battered Japanese compact.

Carver walked to the pizza shop. At the curb were half-a-dozen cars with Par-Cheesey signs on their roofs but only one Japanese compact. Carver stood under the awning and watched the rain drip. The sidewalk traffic surged with going-home activity, with umbrellas going by, faces hidden by the fabric blooms.

24

About fifteen minutes later a middle-aged woman came out carrying a large warming carton stacked with pizzas. The woman put the pizzas into the compact's rear seat, and then scooted behind the wheel. Carver tapped on the glass of the passenger side.

The woman reached over and rolled down the window.

"Hey, friend, I'm in a hurry—"

"Miss Stokes," Carver said, and flashed his ID wallet, "I'd like to talk to you."

"Not now, friend. I'm working—"

"I'll tag along."

Stokes hesitated, looked at her watch, then shrugged and opened the passenger door. Before Carver was settled, the car was jerked into motion.

Stokes was over forty. Forty-five or -six, Carver estimated. About five-four, twenty pounds overweight, but quick in her movements, eyes darting all over, watching traffic.

"So what is this?" Stokes asked. "You a pizza lover? Do I have to fight off the amorous advances of a lust-crazed lover of pizza?"

"No," Carver said, and chuckled. "Poetry and Laura De Anza."

"Just as well. Sex-mad interracial relations would make a lousy liberal theme for a poem. I tried it once—an unpleasant experience. Remind me not to tell you about it."

She had touches of gray peeping from under a shapeless plastic hat. Her speech pattern went up and down the scales, as though she'd had singing instruction long ago.

According to a biographical sketch, she had garnered the acclaim of working women with a series of poems about life in a male-dominated society. Her caustic touch was often compared to W. H. Auden.

"How's the cop business?" Stokes asked.

"I'm not a cop," Carver said, and explained his investigator's status. "I'm helping Laura De Anza."

"So," she said, absorbing the information. She wheeled the car up Grant Avenue. "You're the first one to come along and ask me about that business with Laura. Couldn't figure why the cops didn't talk to me. I heard about her getting

25

arrested on the radio. I don't own a TV. Rots the mind. Why aren't the cops looking and poking around?''

"They're convinced Laura did it.''

"What a bunch of crazies. Typical cop mentality. Laura is emotional and intense, but she's no killer. And she's a hell of a poet. Better than me—maybe. You ever read any of my work?''

"Yes,'' Carver said, and quoted:

> *"The alleys of time become hades*
> *filled with the rattle*
> *of coughing derelict bag ladies—''*

"Dying to make social battle—'' Stokes finished. "Damn, that has to be fifteen years old. You amaze me,'' she said. "I don't meet too many people who actually read poetry. Not mine, anyway.''

"I'm interested in contemporary poetry.''

"Try attending the big poetry read-off.''

"Where?''

"In a couple of nights all the local poets are gathering on board the *Verdugo*, and reading from their works. I'll be there.''

Carver was familiar with the *Verdugo*, a ferryboat from the turn of the century. It had been lovingly restored and was moored at the foot of Polk Street, near Fisherman's Wharf. The boat was a favorite tourist attraction.

"Or,'' Stokes continued, "you can buy my work at City Lights Books. It's the most likely place to get avant-garde poetry. Ferlinghetti has my work there—I don't make much outta that—and I got to make a living, so I deliver pizzas. I'm told by my boss, who's about fifteen years younger than me, that I'm the oldest pizza driver in the city, maybe even in the whole Bay Area.''

Carver said nothing, figuring Stokes would tell him anyway. He was right. She gunned the car up the hill toward Coit Tower and zipped down alleys. Her attention was partly on traffic and tight squeezes between parked cars—but mostly on talking.

"See, poets can't make a living. Unless they're real lucky.

26

I'd be better off writing lyrics to songs, but I could never find the right musical gal. Or guy—

"Besides," she continued, "there's a big difference in the beat. Rhythm you know. The acid in acid rock would probably dissolve my lyrics."

She slammed on the brakes and parked one wheel on the sidewalk.

"Be right back," she said, and grabbed a pizza carton from the warming box on the backseat. She trotted into an apartment building.

Carver looked around. He figured he was on Lombard Street. He waited, the engine running, the wipers *swish-swish*ing. In a couple of minutes Lorna Stokes returned, looked at a notepad, and clashed gears. She stomped on the accelerator, and the little car screamed up Stockton Street.

"Where was I? Oh, yeah. About ten years ago I figured I needed a job that was essentially brainless, so that I can work on my poems in my head."

"Pay any good?"

"No, not at all. See, pizza drivers get minimum wage. And tips. And mileage. It's not too bad, except I got to pay for my own gas and car insurance. But since I'm over twenty-five and don't smoke, my annual premium isn't too bad. But, damn me, those poor kids under twenty-five, their insurance rates are killers and the pizza company doesn't pay for any of that. The public probably thinks the company covers the insurance, but it doesn't." She gave him a quick look. "What do you want to know?"

"What happened at Hatt's?"

"Tell you in a couple minutes," she said, and repeated the performance of delivering a pizza. She was back shortly, shoving dollar bills into her purse.

"Yes, that, at Hatt's . . ." she said when she drove off again. "I been thinking. Just now while delivering hold the onions, heavy on the pepperoni. I guess Laura didn't give the cops my name. Or maybe they don't know where I live. Yeah . . ." Stokes thought for a moment. "Yeah, sure, they don't know where I live. Laura only knows where I work, and she didn't tell them that either."

27

"Apparently not," Carver said.

"Terrific gal, Laura," Stokes said. "Well, last night was one of those evenings where things got off to a bad start. I'd been drinking, something I normally don't do, haven't the stomach for it. And I like to drive at night, I can take care of myself, and the tips are better. Once I had a whole hot box of pizzas stolen from the back of my car. That's bad karma, I can tell you. On them, not me—"

"That night," Carver prodded.

"Like I said, I'd been drinking. And I got into an argument with Geraldine Hare, and Gerry was still pissed at Laura about getting into the book of verse that Yosh—that's Yoshima, Harold Yoshima—peddled to a Tokyo publisher. She tried to get some kind of backing for her own poetry, figuring I don't know why, that Yosh—that's—"

"Harold Yoshima," Carver said.

"Yeah, Yosh—anyway, Gerry had some kind of bug up her ass that a mandate from all the poets in the group could get her poetry into the book. Why the hell she thought that I couldn't tell you."

Carver urged her on.

"Okay, right, so Gerry's plan doesn't work, which wouldn't sway Yosh anyway. I know she had also got a couple of rejections from some magazines that usually accept her. I figure it was too much for her. I tried to console Gerry, to help her, but I used the wrong method. I tried to kid her out of her anger and depression. She didn't take to that at all, and she started calling me names. She slashed her hands at me—God, she had nails on her! I pushed her back, and right about then the other customers joined in and began egging us on."

" 'Fight, Fight, Fight'?" Carver suggested.

"You got it—"

Lorna Stokes parked again and went through her delivery routine. When the car was bumping steeply down Green Street, she picked up her narrative.

Laura De Anza had stepped in and tried to separate the two fighting women. Geraldine Hare turned on Laura, and they yelled at each other. Gerry slapped her and pushed her hard. Laura had stumbled back and fell onto a table, landing on a tureen of minestrone and upsetting plates of spaghetti. Laura had gotten most of the mess on her dress.

"Laura was really pissed," Stokes said. "She probably said things she didn't mean. What really ticked her off was a lot of the other diners laughed. Like Laura was in a slapstick comedy. She's very excitable, you know."

Carver tightened his lips.

"She yelled she'd kill Gerry," Stokes said.

The events agreed with what the waiters had told him. And what Laura had told him. He asked Stokes what happened after that.

"The waiters helped clean off Laura, and Yosh—that's—"

"Yoshima."

"Yeah, anyway he tried to calm her down. But she left Hatt's still steaming."

"Did you notice which way she went?"

"No, I was in a corner with Blue and Bovee. They were trying to calm me down. Which was unnecessary, since I don't hold grudges long. I was almost jovial. Actually I was thi-is close—" She held her index finger and thumb almost touching "—to bursting out laughing myself."

"Had it started to rain when Laura left?"

"No, no rain. That started about fifteen minutes later."

"When did Geraldine Hare leave the restaurant?"

"I guess that was about five minutes after Laura left."

"You're certain?"

"Yeah, I'm sure. We all left about that time. Bovee and Yosh left first, then I guess Blue and Gerry. I left last, and went to work—delivering pizzas."

"Were you driving when the rain began?"

"Not me—I was inside the Par-Cheesey shop. No orders had come in as yet, but in ten minutes, right after the rain started, the cooks were up to their armpits with orders. See, people don't want to go out in the rain, so they call up a pizza place, or a chicken place, or Chinese, any place that delivers."

Which meant, Carver realized, that Lorna Stokes had an alibi. The cooks and cashier and manager of the Par-Cheesey shop would undoubtedly state she was in plain view all the time. A good alibi.

Carver didn't trust it one second. But what possible motive would Stokes have for killing Geraldine Hare?

"What was Hare like?" he asked.

"Not much to say now. She was a damn fine poet. The world was there for her to pluck, to put into succinct words."

"She wasn't married."

"Hell, no. Not her. At least not in the way you mean. She had a lover, a butch. Gerry was a dyke. Didn't effect her poetry much, but once in a while I thought the symbolism got a little heavy. . . ."

Stokes parked again and went off with the last pizza. Carver scrunched down, feeling comfortable inside the trench coat. The interior of the car smelled of warm cheese and spicy tomato and garlicky sausage. He wriggled his toes in his shoes and felt the soles scrape on something gritty.

Suddenly the passenger door was jerked open.

"Get the fuck out, wise ass," a throaty, gravelly voice said, and a hand grabbed Carver's arm. "Come on, hurry it up, Bascombe. You got talkin' to do."

THREE

"Get the fuck outta the car, Bascombe," Detective Sergeant Ernie Ludlow growled. "I ain't goin' to ask twice." The black man's face was practically invisible under the shadow of his hat brim. "Get outta there. We got words."

Carver forced himself to be cool, remain calm, and climbed out of the car. The knot in his stomach remained.

Sergeant Ernie Ludlow gestured for Carver to step along. Drizzle collected on his hat brim and dropped off, spattering the front of the detective's coat.

The drizzle increased and in moments turned to rain. Soft, delicate rain, but rain at any rate. The street's wet garbage smell was added to the smell of hot cheese from Stokes's car, like wash being wrung from a moldy rag.

"What?" Carver asked, once the two men were under an apartment building's front-door canopy.

"Bascombe, just what the fuck do you think you're doin'?"

"Working," Carver replied, and looked idly around for Ludlow's partner, Dan Gulden. There had to be a partner.

"Oh, yeah, sure, sure you are. What're you workin' on?"

"Confidential, Ludlow."

"Sergeant to you, friend. I know it's the Hare killin'. I figure that. And that's way outside your territory. You're messin' in the wrong ball game."

"How'd you find me?"

"I wasn't lookin' for you, nappyhead. You ain't hard to find, if I was lookin' for you, which I ain't."

"For Stokes, then."

"Any dumb dick should figure that. Stokes was easy to find, even though Laura De Anza ain't coppin' out to nothin'. We had it tough diggin' up the info about those other poets."

"They're in the yellow pages," Carver said. "Under P, for poets."

"Bullshit. You'd think those fuckin' poets and poetesses were some kinda celebrities. Most of them ain't in the book—"

"Maybe they can't afford a phone," Carver suggested.

"Yeah? Maybe. Look at this one, Stokes, she's workin' in a pizza joint. Minimum wage, for chrissake. The cashier there told me her route for this order, so I just waited here at the end of her run. And what do I see? You in her car. I figured De Anza hired you. Whatta screwup. Dumbest thing Raf ever did."

"He didn't hire me. Laura's my client."

"Dumber yet. Raf didn't stop her, that's dumb. He couldn't control his woman? Shee-it. He might lose his job over this."

"I don't think you'll be the one to bring charges," Carver said quietly.

He glanced idly into the street shadows for Ludlow's parked car with a partner inside, waiting. No car. At least none in the immediate vicinity.

"Okay, Bascombe, so I'm telling you, stay off this investigation."

Carver said nothing, but shook his head slowly. There was no partner in sight. And on such a dismal night. Carver narrowed his eyes, then relaxed. He had it figured.

"Okay, okay, Bascombe, I know you're one obstinate motherfucker. But I got it here." Ludlow pointed to his temple. "And you know it."

Ludlow was often in a state of anger and agony. The white society he often had to deal with was a pill he detested swallowing. His superiors in the homicide bureau were white, the men at the top echelon of the department were white. Even the reports he had to complete were written on white paper. Ludlow loathed the color.

Ludlow had never learned to accommodate his existence in a white world. He never would; Ludlow considered that selling out. He was determined to beat the honky bastards at their own game.

Because Ernie Ludlow forgot nothing. He had a phenomenal photographic memory. He could recall information and faces like a sophisticated computer.

Lorna Stokes returned to her car, and Ernie Ludlow ordered her over. Ludlow identified himself. After some prodding Stokes repeated to him what she had told Carver.

"Okay," Ludlow said, "that's what I expected to hear. You were there in the pizza joint. The cashier and cook verify that. You know all the other poets, right?"

She admitted she did, and she knew their addresses. Silently frowning, Ludlow held out a notepad and pen. Keeping it from Carver's eyes. Stokes jotted the addresses, and Carver leaned against the canopy support pole.

Why was Ludlow still checking out Laura's story? If the homicide cops had Laura De Anza pegged as the killer, then why was Ludlow still working on the case?

The answer came easy: Sergeant Ernie Ludlow, friend and onetime partner of Raphael De Anza, didn't believe Laura De Anza had killed Geraldine Hare. Damn it, he was still investigating the case! On his own. That's why there was no partner evident.

Which meant Carver and Ludlow were running on a parallel track. Carver nodded; interesting idea. Him and Ludlow together again. Sort of. They hadn't crossed major paths since the Hutte case and the gold thefts.

Ludlow had now eliminated Lorna Stokes as a possible suspect. But what did Ludlow believe? That the poets at Hatt's were the only suspects? There were twelve members of the poetry group—even though only seven had been at Hatt's the previous night.

But since Geraldine Hare's death had occurred away from the restaurant, then any of the twelve-member group might have done it. Or the poets might have had nothing to do with it. It could have been a complete stranger.

Ludlow was finished with Stokes and told her she could leave. She climbed into her car, looked questioningly at Carver, but he shook his head; he'd stay behind. Lorna Stokes drove off in the direction of the Par-Cheesey shop.

"Get outta here," Ludlow ordered Carver.

"I got it pegged," Carver said. "You're trying to help Raf, too."

"Yeah? I am?"

"Yeah. Look, Ernie—"

"Sergeant to you, Bascombe, don't ever forget it. As far as I'm concerned, you're a civilian. You stay out of this."

"Like you? I've been told the cops aren't interested in the others as suspects."

"No? Maybe that's what we want everyone to think. Maybe we just want to get those poets off guard."

"All right. Let's say I believe it. We can share information. If I find out anything I can tell you."

Ludlow laughed, a deep, harsh foghorn laugh.

"Yeah, yeah," Ludlow said, and acted out the motions of wiping crocodile tears from his eyes. "You must think I'm stupid, Bascombe. I've heard plenty of that from you before. You never tell cops shit. You only tell us stuff we're only seconds away from findin' out anyway. Or stuff we already know. Nah, it's a lousy trade. I wouldn't trust you any more than I could wear one a your fancy suits. You want somethin' from me, don't you?"

Carver shrugged.

"I wouldn't give it to you," Ludlow said, "if you handed the killer to me on a platter."

Carver nodded. All right. He would tell Ludlow nothing. But Ludlow had tripped up—he didn't think Laura had killed Geraldine Hare.

"Maybe that's the best way to play it," Carver said. "See you."

Carver turned at the corner and went on down the hill to Broadway. He didn't look back. Sergeant Ernie Ludlow narrowed his eyes at the departing private investigator.

The meeting of Broadway and Columbus Avenue and Grant Avenue was a crossroad of clashing cultures. Grant Avenue was the main street through Chinatown. Where Grant reached the intersection, neon signs in Chinese advertised hotels, shops, restaurants, pharmacies. Kitty-corner from that, Italian North Beach was overloaded with pizza parlors, cappuccino cafés, gelato shops, and mortuaries.

The one movie house on Broadway featured exclusively Chinese movies. Crossing Columbus, that same Broadway was a mass of strip joints.

At Enrico's, Carver ordered coffee. His right foot scraped against the sidewalk, and he slipped the shoe off. Something was embedded in the sole—a small piece of glass. He pried it loose with a penknife. The object was a tiny, curved glass fragment. The inside appeared dark, sooty.

He remembered—he had noticed it in Stokes's car. Just

before Ludlow hauled him out. A thing like that could quickly wear a hole in an expensive shoe.

He finished the coffee and fought the rumblings of his empty stomach. Then Carver telephoned Harold Yoshima. The poet's answering machine didn't click on immediately. Apparently the machine had been turned off, which meant . . . Carver hung up. Yoshima was at home.

The address was five blocks away. Carver was wet and out of breath by the time he had made the steep hike up Montgomery.

The neighborhood was a maze of small streets winding upward toward the top of Telegraph Hill. The fluted column of Coit Tower dominated the hill, a lighted landmark which acted as a gemstone in the coronet of North Beach.

Yoshima lived in one of the myriad small alleys. The air was tinted with the sweet damp smell of night-blooming flowers. Carver entered the building and climbed the stairs to the top floor. Again he turned on his pocket recorder.

He knocked and a medium-built man opened the door. The man's eyes flicked over Carver, widening slightly. From past occasions, Carver figured, he hadn't expected a black man.

"Yes, I'm Yoshima," he said, answering Carver's question. His voice was a rich unaccented baritone.

Yoshima was about forty years old, Carver guessed. In the backlight from the apartment, the man seemed physically fit, with well-modeled musculature showing under a silk shirt, silk tie, and Hopi jacket.

Carver identified himself and briefly explained why he wanted to talk to Yoshima.

"I'm sorry, Mr. Bascombe," Yoshima said, "but I do not wish to speak with you. I am not required to answer any of your questions. Besides—"

"There's going to be a big cop visiting you. An ugly black guy. You won't like him, and I can guarantee you he won't like you."

"I do not see what—"

"Think of my questions as a dress rehearsal. It'd be easier."

"Ah. Perhaps," Yoshima said. He creased his brow in

35

thought. "A dress rehearsal, you say? Yes, I like that. Anything to help Mrs. De Anza." He stroked the silk tie at his throat. "However, I'm somewhat busy at the moment, preparing dinner for myself and a lady friend. Would it be convenient for us to meet later this evening?"

"Yes," Carver said. "I want to talk to Laura's friends in the group. I don't know the addresses of Bovee and Kraft. And you do."

"Of course, and you might use the intervening time to query them. I think that would be most practical." He took out an address booklet from his jacket pocket.

Harold Yoshima rattled off the addresses and phone numbers of Jack Bovee and Holliday Kraft. Carver thanked him and agreed to return at eight-thirty. He walked back down Montgomery Street to Broadway.

Very obliging man, Carver thought.

Why so obliging? Yoshima didn't even ask why Carver was working on the Hare murder.

Again at Enrico's, Carver rewound part of the micro-tape and jotted down the addresses Yoshima had given him. The homicide detectives investigating the case might have given him the addresses, but it would have taken a lot of diplomacy to wheedle the information from them.

Jack Bovee lived near the Art Institute. Royal Blue was many blocks away, on Telegraph Hill. Holliday Kraft's address was in the Golden Gateway—not too shabby for a poet. And fairly close by, with easier parking.

Carver drove down Columbus Avenue, turned onto Montgomery, and parked near the Golden Gateway apartments and condominiums. The lighted buildings sparkled and towered over the dungeon-black financial district.

He found Holliday Kraft's address. In the apartment foyer he pressed the nameplate button. In a few seconds the door buzzed and he went inside, folding his trench coat over one arm. Carver stepped out of the elevator on the fifteenth floor.

Holliday Kraft did all right for herself, Carver thought. She had to have some kind of income other than poetry.

Carver buzzed and the door opened in seconds. A good-looking leggy blonde stood there, a soft, shiny fabric clinging to her curves. Her eyes widened slightly at the sight of the black man at the door, but quickly settled into a languid soft look. Carver caught that halting transition.

"Hello, Tom . . ." she said, caressing the name like it was a valuable fur, "you're a bit early, but come in, please."

"Holliday?" Carver asked.

"Yes," she said, and laughed lightly, a sound of liquid notes. "Come in. I promise I'll—bite."

Carver stepped into the apartment. Honey and wheat were the leitmotif: pale amber drapes, the walls were the color of fields of ripening grain. Soft leather and velour couches and easy chairs. The color of Trojan amber. The lights were dim, adding a subtle touch like candlelight to the rooms. The thick rug was like walking over well-packed oats and barley.

The air was scented with the light odor of lemon. The apartment had the aura of being pleasantly, tastefully edible.

Behind Carver, Holliday Kraft trailed several fingernails across his shoulder blades.

"Let me take your coat, Tom," she said, sliding her fingers over his shoulders and down his lapels. "You're not—not what I thought. In the right light you could almost pass for good-looking. Perhaps you'd care for a drink . . . or do you want something else . . ." Holliday dropped her fingers gently to his crotch and lightly stroked him.

Holliday Kraft was a call girl.

And she thought Carver was a client named Tom. Carver turned and smiled at her.

"No drink, Holliday," he said, "but maybe you can help me."

He took out his wallet—

"That usually comes later," Holliday said. And smiled. "After *you* come, of course."

Then she saw the private investigator's license. A hard look leaped into her eyes then quickly defused.

"A police officer?" she asked. A faint but noticeable tremor had crept into the three words.

"No," Carver said. "Private investigator."

"Ah, I see," she said, sounding instantly relieved. She looked carefully at the identification license. "A PI. I was afraid Lloyd had let something get past him. And your name isn't Tom—Bascombe, Carver Bascombe. What kind of a name is that?"

"My name," Carver said, and sat on a couch.

Holliday sat across from him, a glass-and-brass coffee table between them. She settled into the easy chair like a marshmallow melting into hot chocolate. She smiled tentatively. Carver waited her out.

"Well . . . Carver," she finally said. "What do you want—if not what I usually offer?"

"The police haven't talked to you," Carver said, guessing the answer.

"No," she replied, dragging out the word. "About what?"

A nice, deceitful, innocent act, Carver thought. And not too well done.

"About Geraldine Hare—about Laura De Anza."

"Oh. That was a terrible thing to happen. I thought I knew Laura, thought I knew her fairly well, but I guess you just can't tell about people, can you?"

Carver nodded. He didn't like her act, didn't trust it for a second. Not because she was a prostitute. Her words sounded as if she had learned them in a college freshman course in Dramatic Arts 1A.

He wondered what she really thought. And he didn't doubt for a moment that she thought hard and deep.

"Laura didn't do it," he said. "So I'm looking for the right answer."

"Why are you telling me?"

"Why not? You're smart. You probably know things you don't want anyone to know about."

"Which things could you possibly mean?"

"I can think of two things right off. One—you wouldn't want your business colleagues to know you write poetry—and second—you might not want your poet friends to know you fuck for a living."

"Ah, shock tactics. I'm disappointed in you. I thought you might do better. Actually I don't give a damn who knows

38

what I do. Scribbling poetry or laying on my back. It's what I do."

"Are you any good?" Carver asked, and quickly added, "at poetry?"

"You mean you came up here to see me, to interr-o-gate me, and you didn't research me at all? I think that's a shame. It shows a lack of preparation on your part. I think a good detective would come fully prepared with inside information. Don't you think so? Wouldn't you agree with me on that?"

"I'm not about to incriminate myself."

Holliday Kraft laughed, a pleasant, musical sound, which carried the false quality of only originating from her throat. Again, a practiced affectation.

"However," Carver added,

> *"Roses are now strewn*
> *scattered in windows*
> *scenting our bedroom*
> *and my lovesmell glows—"*

"Oh, good. I'm impressed. You don't look like the type who reads poetry. Wouldn't a police blotter, or whatever they call it, be more your milieu?"

"Police blotters went out ages ago."

"I, of course, didn't know that. I've never been involved with the police. Not once. Never. Isn't that remarkable?"

"Wonderful," Carver said. "Lloyd sees to that."

"I don't think I'll answer that. It might incriminate me."

"What did you do after the fight at Hatt's?" he asked.

"Now that's what I call an abrupt change of subject."

"Yeah. I'm interested."

"I came home, right here, and worked on a poem. A lovely poem about flowers and people sailing toy boats in the park."

"Your pimp wasn't here?"

"Oh, dear, I don't think I like the sound of that. I don't have a pimp, as you call him."

"Lloyd. Whatever you call him."

"Lloyd is my business manager. We're incorporated, and

he takes care of the financial arrangements. Just like any other corporation.''

"Yeah," Carver said. "What do you think of Laura De Anza?"

"Changing the subject again, aren't you? Is that some kind of terribly clever interrogation technique?"

"About Laura . . ."

"Oh, I think she killed Gerry. I'm sure she did."

FOUR

Carver Bascombe rubbed a hand over his jaw. His index finger played with the indentation in his chin. He studied Holliday Kraft, trying to figure what made her tick—other than greed. She was good at role-playing. Was the real Holliday only found in her poems? Or was she as shallow as she made herself out to be?

Whoever she really was, deep down, she wasn't going to let anyone reach her. She'd had a lot of practice at evasion.

"Why do you think she killed Hare?" Carver finally asked.

"She's got that Latin temperament. She's capable of killing someone just like so many people like her."

Carver held his tongue. Let her keep talking, he told himself. Don't get angry over such stupid statements.

"Besides," Holliday said, "according to the newspapers the police are already convinced Laura committed the crime. So why should the police continue looking for the killer?

Otherwise they would've been here questioning me, trying to find out what I knew, and possibly even, heaven forbid, suspecting me of committing murder. Isn't that so?''

Carver shrugged, moving his shoulder a bare quarter of an inch.

"Actually I liked Laura," Holliday said. "We were friends. But I don't think I have anything to worry about, do you?''

"One cop isn't convinced," Carver said. "He's a mean one. Name's Ludlow. You won't like him much."

"Ooh, I'm scared to death. Maybe I should call Lloyd. He's a personal friend of the mayor. Isn't it nice to know people who are in a position to help one in a difficult position?''

"Yeah," Carver replied, reflecting on her deliberate use of the word "position."

"Wait right there, Carver," Holliday said, and rose from the easy chair, the movement practiced and sensual. "I'll be right back. I'm just going to get several books of my lovely poems. Just for you. A gift for you."

She trailed her hand lightly over his arm. A lemon fragrance followed in her wake. Carver watched her disappear into a spacious room. He could make out the corner of a large linen-covered table, probably a dining-room table. She was gone for about two minutes. When Holliday returned, she carried several slim books in one hand. And a palm-sized automatic pistol in the other.

She handed Carver the books and sat again in the easy chair. Casually she laid the small pistol on the arm of the chair.

"Privately printed," she said, indicating the books in Carver's hand. "But previously published in many magazines. I got paid for all of them. Which doesn't happen to many of the poets in our group. I do hope you find my work of some interest—but please don't return to tell me your opinion. I'm really not the least bit interested."

"Then why give them to me?"

"Because, looking at you, I'd guess that you believe true artists reveal much of themselves in their art. And I agree with that. You're the type who'll study the people who are in our poetry group through their art."

"Are you attending the poetry reading on the *Verdugo*?"

"No, I'm not. I was not invited. I am not considered modern enough, not avant-garde enough."

"I was hoping we might—"

"I don't think so, Carver. Disabuse yourself of that notion."

He grinned a tiny bit. But she was right about one thing— if poems were anything, they were a clue to the deep inner character of the writers. Assuming they wrote from the heart and soul.

Some do. Some don't.

A liar might be revealed by words.

"Holliday, what kind of a person was Geraldine Hare?"

"A nice person, but emotional. Actually one of the better-known poets in the United States. She'd been published in many universities' literary magazines, and in the *Atlantic* magazine, and twice in the *New Yorker* magazine. I think it was a mean trick of Yosh's not putting Gerry in his volume of poetry."

"I'll read these," Carver said, indicating the books she had given him. "Maybe we can discuss them at another time?"

"Please don't bother," Holliday Kraft said softly, but bore down on each syllable for emphasis. "I mean it. Don't return." She fondled the automatic pistol casually. The barrel pointed more or less in his direction. "As you might guess, I can take care of myself. So please don't come back. I've had my first experience with a private detective, and I don't wish to repeat it."

Carver thanked Holliday and left the apartment.

A good-looking man was looking at the lobby cards.

"Fifteenth floor, Tom," Carver said, taking a wild guess. The man turned and looked quizzically at him.

"Do I know you?" he asked.

Carver shook his head and grinned. Several minutes later he found a parking space about two blocks from Yoshima's apartment house. He spent a few minutes going over some of Yoshima's published poetry. He quickly memorized one haiku.

As Carver approached the address, he noticed a young black woman leaving the building. She had a pleased smile, as though she had recently enjoyed herself.

Was this Harold Yoshima's lady guest? It was possible.

The young woman paid no attention to Carver as she walked past. A scent drifted in the air as she went by. Jean Patou 1000, Carver guessed. Expensive stuff. He couldn't make out much of her face, since an umbrella hid most of it, and she wore a shapeless rain hat. He climbed the stairs to the top floor and rang the apartment bell.

"Please come in, Mr. Bascombe," Harold Yoshima requested.

The apartment was neat and spare, with tatami mats on most of the floors. Grass cloth covered the walls of the living room, and sliding shoji screens created a feeling of distance from the hectic world outside.

As he stood in the foyer, Carver put his knitted cap in his coat pocket. He caught a scent of perfume lingering in the air. Jean Patou 1000. Off to one side was a closet with the door ajar. Yoshima asked for Carver's trench coat, and when he put the coat in the closet, Carver glimpsed a pale robe and several dark-colored fabric belts.

"Want me to take my shoes off?" Carver asked.

"No," Yoshima said, and chuckled lightly. "Despite the obvious decor of the apartment, I do not follow all the customs of my grandfather's homeland."

Carver looked past a fractionally open shoji screen into what was obviously a workroom. The glow of several computer screens cast a greenish light onto the translucent screens.

Yoshima guided Carver into the front room where they sat on low couches. A lacquer table between them had coffee in a pot and a decanter of vodka at the side. Yoshima offered them, and Carver agreed to a cup of coffee.

The rising aroma of coffee masked most of the perfume smell. Yoshima was apparently unaware of the faintly hovering, enticing scent.

Carver took the offered cup and Harold Yoshima sipped his own coffee and gazed at his guest.

"Now, Mr. Bascombe, I apologize for my rudeness at our first meeting. I was most reluctant to speak to you. I think you can understand my trepidation. Geraldine's death is still somewhat of a shock. And for Laura to be arrested . . . what is it you wish to know?"

"Your impression of the fight between Geraldine Hare and Lorna Stokes."

Yoshima nodded and gave a brief, unemotional description of the affair. The story was a duplicate of everything Carver had already heard. Nothing new there.

"I've now answered your question—perhaps you'll oblige me by reciprocating. This is a police affair, and a prime suspect had been arrested. Why you are investigating this murder case?"

Carver gave a brief explanation of being hired by Laura De Anza to find someone who saw her and could alibi her.

"I see," Yoshima said, and stroked his throat and necktie. "I know nothing of the murder, of course, and obviously you do not believe Laura guilty. What are your chances of success, Mr. Bascombe?"

"Good."

"Ah, I like that—a confident man. I assume you've used the past hours interviewing others?"

"Yes—Lorna Stokes and Holliday Kraft."

"And?"

"I still have a few to see. Tell me about Geraldine Hare."

"A capable poet," Yoshima replied.

"That's all? Just capable?"

"Yes, that is sufficient, I believe."

"You didn't select her to be in your anthology."

"No, I did not." Yoshima finished his coffee, and then poured a dollop of vodka into the cup. He drank, then looked at Carver. "I shall explain, Mr. Bascombe. Although I do not ordinarily feel that I must defend my actions or my decisions."

Carver made a polite gesture for him to continue.

"I wanted not only the best poets from the group, but other

44

poets from other regions in the United States. From that point of view alone, I would have to leave many competent poets out. I wanted only the best—and I admit it is based on personal opinion.''

"Go on," Carver said.

"Geraldine is good. Above mediocre, but just so. Not aesthetically pleasing to myself. Another factor—a heavily weighted one—is that the poets had to be fresh, relatively unknown, particularly to the publisher and to the readers in Japan. Geraldine Hare has—excuse me—had an established reputation. When I agreed to be the editor of this book, it was understood it would be based on my personal choices. Obviously, anyone in my position would displease someone. Is this not so?''

"Yeah, it's the name of the game.''

"Allow me to state the current feelings about the composing of poetry. We see it as a musical rhythm, rather than the old-fashioned mechanical meter, measured against a counting of syllables—so many syllables to a line.

"Rhythm is appreciated mostly when it reflects the emotion of the poet against the subject he or she is working on. There has to be a knowledge, the beauty of the emotion expressed. A poem is an art, an artistic object unto itself. It is a reality unto itself, and as such we do not think it is an imitation of reality, it is reality.''

Carver nodded.

"Form is a way we have of weighing and measuring content,'' Yoshima continued. "There are many measurements. For instance, *melopoeia*, the music sound of the poem, the way the ear hears it. Perhaps you are familiar with others?''

Carver said he was, but he realized it had been a long time since he had studied poetry in college.

"Miss Hare lacks much of these measurements. I rejected her work for some of her stylisms, but mostly because she was too well known. Naturally Geraldine was incensed. She felt that all the poets in our group should be in the book. Especially as she had built a reputation in the literary world. To me that meant nothing.''

45

Carver wondered if Harold Yoshima wished he'd never started the project.

"I think," Yoshima continued, "the exposure for new American poets in Japan will be of enormous benefit. Already there is an American publisher eager to be first in the bidding for the American rights."

"Are you about finished with the project?"

"Almost. In a day or so. As with any book, it is in a mock-up state. A dummy copy. Then I shall deliver it in person to the publisher. It's much too valuable to trust to the mails."

"Flying, of course," Carver said.

"No, I have a great fear of flying. I see those great behemoths in the sky—and I think to myself, it is impossible for them to stay up there. But then murder is impossible to my mind. And it has happened." He rubbed his throat.

"Do you think Laura De Anza killed Geraldine Hare?"

"I'm sorry for her," Yoshima said. "I think it was a terrible thing to do."

"So you believe she did it?"

"The police believe so. Who am I to counter their official stance? I have no information to give them to prove otherwise. I wish I had. I'd like to help Laura."

He stroked his throat, then the knot of his tie. He poured himself another vodka.

"But," he continued, "I don't think I can foresee the circumstances under which I could be of much help."

"What kind of person was Hare?"

"I do not wish to speak ill of the dead."

"Which is another way of saying there is something ill to be said."

"Perhaps."

"Okay," Carver said. "Back to Laura De Anza—do you believe she is capable of committing murder?"

"Which is not the same question as asking if she did indeed commit the killing." Yoshima stroked a fingernail against the knot of his tie. "Yes, it is possible. Laura is a volatile woman. She has much dark fire and emotion in her poetry. Too much perhaps, but it is poetry of great beauty

46

and passion. For that reason, perhaps, she was not adept at haiku." He looked at Carver. "You are familiar with haiku, perhaps?"

"Yes," Carver said, nodding. "A simple form of three lines and usually seventeen syllables—five, seven, five—in those three lines. Rhyming is not a necessity. The structure is more important, and the content. Haiku concerns itself with man's relationship with the natural world. You're supposed to be an artist at it."

"Others have said so," Yoshima admitted almost apologetically.

Carver reluctantly admired the man's studied humility. But he had already seen the pale robe and the brown and black belts hanging in the closet.

"Haiku takes a meditative mind," Carver said, and quoted:

> *"Mantis a green leaf*
> *waits and prays for meals*
> *garden camouflage."*

"Thank you," Yoshima said. "I'm flattered. Haiku requires a disciplined mind. Occasionally a humorous or mocking mind."

"And you don't believe Laura is like that?"

"Not when she is writing poetry. And poetry is a window to the soul. Not a window of glass, not a craft, but an art, a private art of writing. A deep, highly honed art of communication. It is the reason why greeting-card poetry is so despised. There is no belief there, only commercial sentimentality."

"Where were you when Geraldine Hare was killed?"

"I was with a friend," Yoshima said. "another of the poets—Jack Bovee."

"A good alibi."

"I don't consider it as such, with its implication that I need some kind of protective umbrella—but it is the truth. We were together, walking along Broadway, enjoying the bright lights, as we often do."

47

"Why often?"

"Jack is my coeditor of the book of poetry—which has apparently been the cause of the death of Geraldine Hare."

"I suppose someone other than Jack Bovee saw you?"

"I haven't the faintest idea. I don't recollect that we stopped and chatted with anyone. I think I saw Lawrence Ferlinghetti in Enrico's . . . but I don't believe he saw me."

"A homicide detective named Ludlow will visit you, and he'll ask you much the same questions."

"Thank you, Mr. Bascombe, for that information. I'll use our conversation as a first-draft rehearsal."

"Sergeant Ernie Ludlow—he's a hard case."

"An interesting phrase," Harold Yoshima said. "One definition of a case is of an object which contains a well-defined and limited amount of space."

He said that musingly, as though he might be interested in testing Ludlow's strength and intelligence.

"Now then, Mr. Bascombe, perhaps you'll satisfy more of my curiosity. What are your next plans? What do you do next?"

FIVE

Carver Bascombe left the apartment building. The rain continued, and he shoved his cap on his head. He thrust his hands into the deep, warm pockets of his trench coat and headed for his parked car.

Yoshima had told Carver where he worked—at East Wind Process, a computer company in Silicon Valley, about forty-five minutes south, in Santa Clara County. Carver in turn gave him several of his business cards.

One question still nagged Carver: If Laura De Anza didn't kill Geraldine Hare—who else had a motive and what was it? However, that was hardly his problem. Soon, either he or Bea Murphy or Tettsui would find someone who had seen Laura the previous evening.

The search for her alibi was only the beginning. Carver couldn't keep his hands off the case. Even if he found Laura's alibi—well, there wasn't anything that said he couldn't find the killer.

And wouldn't it be nice to upstage Ludlow? A warm glow fed off the thought. A deep fire within warmed the hunter's hands.

The rain kept the streets relatively empty. Carver was tired and felt hungry. He had one more stop to make—Royal Blue—and then he'd go home and fix something hot. He'd start out fresh in the morning. Unless his sleep got interrupted by one of the PIs on the job tonight.

Deep in thought, he passed an alley. Two men left the rainy darkness of the passage and fell into step behind Carver. They matched his measured pace, their footsteps sloshing on the wet sidewalk. But they were clumsy and eager. Carver heard their rapid footsteps gaining on him.

He whipped around, on the balls of his feet, his hands out of his pockets and ready.

Not good enough.

The first man, medium-sized, threw a fist against Carver's shoulder. The blow twisted Carver off-balance. The second man, a monster about Carver's height but heavier, slammed a fist into Carver's jaw.

Rolling fast, dizzy, shaking his head, Carver threw himself away from the two men. He needed time! He skidded into a crouch, his hands formed into slashing slabs.

Odd. He smelled chocolate.

The medium-sized one wore a leather jacket, which

49

gleamed wetly from the streetlights. Carver measured off the distance in an instant and slashed his right hand into the man's throat.

The guy in leather grunted. Unfazed. The only other sounds were of heavy breathing. No cursing, no shouts; only the intense serious calm of combat.

The monster, wearing a red windbreaker, swung a knobby blackjack against Carver's skull. Carver's cap absorbed some of the numbing blow. The guy then wrapped muscular arms around Carver's chest. He had him in a bear hug from behind. Carver smelled chocolate again. The big guy had been eating candy. Carver stomped on the monster's instep and felt the arms loosen.

For a fraction of a second.

The one in the leather jacket slugged Carver in the belly. Carver gasped and threw a fist at the guy's face. Satisfyingly, he felt the jolt up through his knuckles. The guy staggered back.

The monster holding him, breathing heavily, let go of one arm and chopped a short right into Carver's temple. Glittery bursts and whirls! Carver thought he'd blacked out! Only for a moment!

He had.

The two men had him now, braced against the nearest building. Monster candy-eater had him by the throat and hit him repeatedly in the chest. Leather jacket alternated with several fast fists to the jaw.

Carver's head was bashed to the right, then to the left. His blood splattered the wall on either side of him.

A few more blows and he was released. He slid to the wet pavement. The monster in the red windbreaker knelt and grabbed a handful of Carver's hair. He jerked Carver's face into the falling rain.

"Wake up, nigger," the man said, almost kindly, as though he were talking to a naughty pickaninny.

"Ulmph," Carver said, and tried to lift his eyelids.

"That's better," the man said. "Listen up. What you're doing is why we're taking you out. You want more we'll be glad to come back and do it again. If you don't want more—then drop whatever it is you're doing."

"In other words," leather jacket said, "dump the case. Forget the job. Personally I think—hey, wake up—"

Carver blinked and licked his bloody lips. His ribs ached and his lungs were on fire with every breath.

"Right, right," leather jacket continued, "that's better. I think you're one hell of a stand-up guy. But you're outta your class against us. Keep up the snooping and we'll drop you straight."

The guy in the red windbreaker stood and talked for a moment with his partner. The guy unwrapped a candy bar and threw the wrapper on the sidewalk. After a minute, he returned and kicked Carver in the ribs.

"That's it, nigger," the big chocoholic said, "for now, anyway. Remember what we said. Drop it. Next time you won't like us any better."

Carver slumped to one side, sliding a few inches down the inclined pavement. He lay there for long moments and slowly gathered his breath.

In the next few minutes, on the opposite side of the narrow street, two pedestrians hurried by. No help there. Carver finally struggled upright, using the buildings for support. He staggered to his car, jingling the ignition keys from his pocket.

Two of the Chrysler's tires were slashed.

Carver shook his head slowly. What the hell. This was getting bad. Slowly he dragged himself to the driver's side and unlocked the door. He crawled in and sagged against the seat. He breathed hard, his eyes closed.

He opened his lids and unclipped the cellular telephone. He tapped out a number, and Jimmy Bowman answered.

"I need help," Carver said.

"What's up, Cahvah?" his friend asked.

"Got two tires slashed. Need them fixed."

"You don't sound good, Cahvah."

"No."

Jimmy Bowman asked, and Carver told him his location.

Bowman said he'd be there in fifteen minutes, hold tight. Carver grunted and hung up.

Anger replaced pain. Awakened were ten thousand years of Masai hunters that stalked in the cold shadow of Kilimanjaro. The hunt—along the Olduvai Gorge—

Carver Bascombe reached into his shirt pocket and removed the mini-cassette recorder. It was still functioning. Hadn't been shut off after leaving Yoshima's apartment. Carver rewound the tape and played back the street attack—

"Listen up. What you're doing is why we're taking you out. You want more we'll be glad to come back and do it again. If you don't want more—then drop whatever it is you're doing."

Drop it. Message understood. Fuck you, Carver thought. Nobody tells him what to do. What was it Maya Angelou wrote? *Don't let nobody tell you nothing.* That's right, Maya. Nobody.

But what the hell was going on? Who stuck the two guys on him?

Carver retraced the day's events: couldn't have been anyone he'd interviewed on Nob Hill. They were chosen and talked to at random. Possibly, but not likely, hired by one of the waiters at Hatt's.

Had to have been one of the poets he'd seen.

Lorna Stokes, who had a lot to say. All on tape.

Holliday Kraft, who had a lot to say. And at gunpoint. She was the only one who'd told him not to come back.

Harold Yoshima, who corroborated most of what others had already said. Did he have the time to call a couple of thugs?

The one person who had something to lose—and someone to back it up—

Yeah. Carver's eyes widened. He was sure he knew who had sent the two grunts.

"What you got here is a problem," Jimmy Bowman said, and kicked at one of the two slashed tires.

Bowman was a small man, wiry, with a dusting of freckles across the cheeks and bridge of his mellow-brown face. His eyes were usually sparked with devilment, but now they were serious, filled with concern for his friend.

"But, Cahvah, not to fret," Bowman said to his friend. "Knowing this car as I do, like a buddy, I brought along a couple of replacements. Several of Akron, O-hi-o's best." He wiped his hands on his rain-streaked white coveralls. "Take only a few bits to jack up this motha and replace them."

He looked at Carver, who leaned against the Chrysler's hood. The car and the wet pavement glistened under the flashing yellow light of Bowman's tow truck.

"Yeah, man, you don't look so good," Bowman continued. "Tell you what, you get into the truck, and I'll change the tires. Then we'll tow the car to your place. You don't look fit enough to drive. That okay with you?"

"No, Jimmy," he said, "thanks, but I've got one more place to go. . . ."

"Man, you crazy, you know that."

"It's close by . . . a few blocks . . ."

"You got that determined sound again in your voice . . . but okay, but don't say I never told you you got a concussion, 'cause I think you do."

"Jimmy, I don't think I have a concussion—but if I do, it's a mild one."

"Yeah, blackjacks do that to you."

Bowman finished changing the slashed tires. He was deeply concerned for his friend.

"Shit, man, you just gotta be some kinda tough guy, don't you?"

"Nobody pushes me off," Carver said, and slid behind the wheel of the Chrysler.

"Oh, yeah, I hear that. I can hear your ribs gratin' too. Bet you got a cracked rib or two. Maybe even busted."

"Yeah. Know what's worse?"

"What, Cahvah?" Bowman asked worriedly.

"They ruined an expensive suit."

He gunned the accelerator and drove off. Bowman shook his head morosely. Several minutes later Carver parked on

53

the crest of Kearney Street, at the steep intersection of Green Street.

Royal Blue. Carver nodded to himself; he'd wanted to meet this woman for a long time. He enjoyed her poetry; it was tough and original. She lived at the end of the block, the apartment on the fourth floor.

He straightened his trench coat and suit, and cleaned himself as best he could with a handkerchief. Had to make himself presentable.

He went up the stairs, fighting back the pain that seared his ribs. He ignored the twisted knots that pulsed at his temples. He forced his attention to the decor, admiring the thirties Art Deco—rounded corners of glass blocks, fanlight windows with frosted etched figures of modern gazelles and modern streamlined fish.

At the top of the stairs Carver stopped. He forced himself not to stare.

The door to Royal Blue's apartment hung twisted in its frame, hanging by one bent bottom hinge. The frame around the lock was splintered. The door had been kicked open. The dark rooms beyond were a mess, shadowy uptilted chairs, wall pictures askew . . .

"Don't . . . don't move," a woman's voice behind him whispered. "I'll kill you. . . . I swear I will. . . ."

Trembling and fear was layed over the voice. The sound was vulnerable, quavering.

Carver slowly raised his hand. A scent—familiar, enticing—touched him. Jean Patou 1000. He half turned to the voice behind him. In the shadows of the stair landing he made out a hand holding a small revolver.

He continued the turn.

> "Roses are red," he said.
> "Violets are blue.
> And you must be Royal Blue."

"What?" the voice quavered.
Carver faced her; he could not see her clearly.

"I'm going to reach for my identification. Easy with that thing, all right?"

He brought out his ID wallet.

"Are you the police?" the woman asked, as she squinted from the darkness. "I didn't call the police."

"Not the city police," he said. "Private investigator. Carver Bascombe. Let's go inside."

"I . . . I don't know. . . ."

Royal Blue was scared stiff and needed support.

"Follow me in if you want," he said.

Carver stepped into her apartment. He flicked on a lamp. Yeah, the apartment was a mess. Furniture on its side, papers from a desk strewn over the hardwood floor, the desk itself upside down, one leg broken off. Framed prints had been knocked off the walls; broken glass crunched underfoot. The air had a cold, wet feel.

Carver looked around. Several of the windows had been broken, and the damp air whistled through the rooms. The effect was meant to frighten. None of the chairs had been sliced open, no pillows torn apart. Someone merely went through the apartment tipping things over, breaking glass.

The cracked mirror over the fireplace mantel had a message written redly, smearily, with a lipstick.

Royal Blue stepped across the threshold, her eyes darting from side to side, both hands clenching the handgun. Carver turned casually and smiled. He noted the weapon: a two-inch Smith & Wesson revolver. A .32. Not much of a weapon, but it'd put a hole through anyone's heart or brain.

She was gorgeous. Even in her fright, he thought. Dark brown skin, of a quality that suggested dark forest trees. Her fear-ridden eyes were the color of rich, loamy earth, with long lashes like riverbank ferns.

Carver guessed her to be in her late twenties.

Her fear brought out a sense of color under her skin which made her face glow.

Her black hair seemed iridescent, as though clustered with hidden electrical energy. Her nerves were like dust—about to fly away if anything else occurred. It wouldn't take much, Carver thought. One more incident and she'd crack wide open.

"They seem to have done a good job," Carver said, keeping his tone nonchalant, nonthreatening. "Any idea who did it? Or why?"

Royal shook her head. Trembling.

"There's nothing missing—but my own home invaded—ugh! I feel dirty—dirty inside. I feel helpless. I feel like screaming, but there's nothing to scream against."

"You're supposed to feel that way," Carver said.

"Buy why?"

"You know something, Royal, or someone thinks you know something. It's a way to terrorize you. Keep you quiet. Make you feel vulnerable, that you can be gotten to."

"They're doing it all right." She held herself tighter and shuddered. "I'm scared—more scared than I've ever been in my life. You're right . . ." she said, her voice small, "it's what I know. About the murders—"

"Murders? Plural?"

"Yes. Two murders." She looked at him, her lips compressed. "Geraldine Hare was not the first . . . not the first to die. She was the second poet . . . the second female poet who's been murdered." She shuddered. "And I'm the third. I'm next."

SIX

"I'm sorry—" Royal Blue stammered, "but I don't remember your name? I'm so nervous."

He told her and asked her to explain what she had meant about two murders.

"What happened to you," she asked, evading his question. "Your clothes? You look like you've been in a fight or something."

He nodded without answering her. Obviously she needed moral support. He picked up a telephone from the floor—fighting back the pain from grating ribs—and tapped out Bea Murphy's beeper number. He gave the paging service Royal Blue's number.

He looked at her and smiled, to give her a psychological boost. He called a second number and reached Peaches Boone, the carpenter who had done much of the major work in remodeling the Victorian house and bringing it up to code. Peaches said she'd be there in fifteen minutes.

"Who did you call?" Royal asked.

"Paging service," he said, and went into the kitchen and sorted out the items for making coffee. "For a private investigator—a woman. The second call was to a carpenter who'll fix up some of this mess. At least board up the doors and windows."

She said nothing, just held the gun at her side and waited for the coffee to finish perking.

"You're doing a lot for me," Royal said finally, "and I gave you a bad time."

"That's all right. I knew what time it was."

She chuckled despite her shivers. But she still held the S & W.

Carver poured steaming coffee into two cups and handed one to Royal Blue. In the living room he began to straighten up the mess. His head throbbed each time he bent over.

There was another possibility—that a bug had been planted in the apartment. Unlikely but something to consider. Perhaps someone wanted to know who Royal Blue would call for help.

"Tell me about tonight," he asked.

"I had a dinner date—with a friend—"

"Harold Yoshima," he said.

"Oh," she said, her great brown eyes wide. The gun came up to hip level. "How did you know that?"

"I saw you leaving his place. I had an appointment to talk to him. About a good friend of mine—Laura De Anza."

"You know Laura? Oh, she's a dear friend. I'm sorry she's in such trouble—"

"I'm helping her," he said, and then the telephone rang.

Carver picked it up. He identified himself to Bea Murphy.

"What's up, Carver?" she asked.

"A problem," he said, and gave her a brief rundown of the situation—and Royal's address. "She could a use woman's touch, Bea."

"Go on, you chauvinist. I'll be there in ten minutes, lad. Or less."

Carver hung up and then urged Royal Blue to continue her story. As she talked, Royal picked up her portable typewriter and locked it in its case.

"After dinner with Yosh I didn't come right home. It was raining nicely—I love the rain—so I just went for a walk. First up to Coit Tower. I looked out over the bay. It's beautiful, with the bridge lit up, glistening in the rain. I often go there. It helps with my writing—I walked some more and then I walked home—to this—and I was just sick."

She moved around the apartment, straightening up furniture, picking up vases, books. Etcetera. Carver swept up the glass. He put a ceramic cat back on the fireplace mantel.

"I was petrified—and I got this gun I own," she continued, and looked at the weapon, as if surprised to see it still in her hand. "I can't really say what I thought I was going to do with it, but I felt protected. The people downstairs are away for the week, so I guess no one heard the person who broke in."

He nodded. She was so lovely—he couldn't keep from watching her. She paused and realized he was watching her. She looked at him. Did she smile? Carver thought. A tiny smile?

"I stood in all this—this vandalism," she said, "and then I heard someone coming up the stairs. So I hid outside. You came up."

"Yeah," he said.

"It's what's so horrible about it. All this—to frighten me. As if I wasn't frightened enough about two murders—"

"*Damn it*, Carver, lad," Bea Murphy said, and stepped over the debris of the wrecked door, "haven't you learned to knock? Don't be so impetuous with your lady friends."

Despite his aches, Carver chuckled and introduced Royal Blue.

"It's nice to meet new people," Bea said to Royal, and added, "especially those who are still living. Who died? Unless I didn't hear right as I walked in."

"Later, Bea," Carver said. "Right now we need a safe place for her. We're just waiting for Peaches Boone to show up."

"Sure, lad—it'll be good to see Peaches again."

Bea wondered briefly why Carver wouldn't take a woman in distress to his house—and then chided herself for such an unkind thought. Carver had his reasons, and they were usually correct. She looked at Carver's clothes and shook her head dolefully.

"Ah, look at that, your suit. What did you do, Carver,

slip in the rain? Or did one of them poets bowl you over with an iambic pentameter?'' She turned to Royal Blue and picked up a purse and handed it to Royal. "Don't worry, dear, you'll need this. Leave everything to us. All your doors—and windows—will be stronger than ever."

Carver took Bea aside and spoke in a low voice.

"We've got to assume the possibility this apartment has been bugged. Remember the place where we were three weeks ago—where you spilled coffee on stakeout—?''

"Oh, sure,'' Bea said.

"We're putting Royal there."

"You're not telling the cops about this?''

"I'm not telling them anything."

He had made an offer—sort of—to Ludlow and had gotten rejected for his troubles. So be it, he thought.

"All right, dear,'' Bea said, turning to Royal Blue, "things are moving. Put the gun away, dear—in your purse is fine—then while we wait for Miss Peaches Boone, why, we can just fix things up a mite."

After a few minutes clumping sounds came from the stairwell, and Peaches Boone walked through the door. She was a big woman, a no-nonsense type. She wore overalls, with her thumbs hooked into the top. She made clucking sounds at the damage but told them it was not so bad. She'd get some plywood from her pickup truck and board up the door and then cover the windows.

Carver nodded and knew Royal's apartment was in good hands. He clicked off his recorder and asked Royal to pack an overnight bag.

A few minutes later, with Bea Murphy carrying Royal's typewriter, they were on their way to a motel on Lombard Street.

"Now, dear,'' Bea said to Royal, "you can tell us all about this other murder."

Royal Blue looked worriedly at Carver.

"It's okay,'' Carver said, and surreptitiously turned on the recorder.

"You can talk in front of me,'' Bea said to Royal. "I have a more sympathetic attitude than the Great White Hunter here. But don't let those rugged looks fool you. Beneath that slim, dangerous-looking black man, who likes to think he has a steel-trap mind, is a very dangerous black man with the mind of a grizzly-bear trap. What about this murder?"

"It's true," Royal said. "Geraldine Hare was the second murder victim. I can't prove it, but I believe it."

She had regained her composure, was more in control of herself. She spoke clearly, her voice musical and rhythmic.

"Go ahead," Carver said, turning onto Van Ness Avenue.

"The first death took place about two weeks ago—her name was Olive Dale, and she wrote poetry under the name of Olive Beem Dale. Her maiden name had been Beem. Gordon Dale, the architect, is her husband. Was. She didn't belong to the poetry group, but Yoshima had asked her to join—"

"Why?" Carver asked.

"Because Geraldine Hare had threatened to quit unless her poetry was included in Yosh's anthology."

"How'd she die, dear," Bea asked.

"She was found behind her apartment, in the alley. The police decided she was drunk and fell from her balcony. . . . They labeled it an accident."

"And you think otherwise."

"Yes, I do. So does her husband."

"Why, dear?" Bea asked.

"Because the police said she fell because Olive was drunk. They said her blood showed a high concentration of alcohol. They figured she probably staggered onto the balcony and fell over."

Carver interrupted, told Royal to hold her thoughts, and pulled into the motel on Lombard Street. The motel owner, Mr. Nedden, was a client of Carver's security business; he was glad to help since employee theft had dropped by a third. Decreased vandalism had lowered his insurance premiums and saved him several times Carver's fee.

"Safe as houses," Bea Murphy said, once they were in their rooms. "For you, lad, Nedden won't even register the lady until tomorrow. For now, it's a vacant suite. I've got connecting rooms next door."

Royal dropped her overnight bag on the bed and took out her typewriter and placed it on the desk. She arranged several paperback books and a short stack of paper next to the typewriter.

"Okay, Royal, go on," Carver urged.

"I knew Olive," Royal said, sounding stronger, less afraid. "She was an old friend of mine. She was a poet who often helped me with my problems in meter or subject matter—you see, in my writing—"

"Don't disgress," Carver said bluntly. "Why do you think she was pushed?"

"Olive didn't drink. She was a diabetic. A sort of borderline case—she didn't inject insulin with a hypodermic—"

"She took micronase?"

"Yes, that was it. A small pill to control her blood sugar. She hardly ever drank liquor. It would have turned into sugar and put her into a coma. She told me drinking might ultimately lead to her having to use injections. She hated the idea of doing that."

Carver nodded and rubbed a finger into the cleft in his chin.

"All right," he said, "but the cops didn't buy any of that?"

"No. Not at all. But if Olive had a high alcohol level, then someone put it in her."

"Forced her, you mean?" Bea said.

"Yes. I think so," Royal said in a low whispery voice. "I believe it had to happen like that. But the investigating team said that a lot of diabetics often denied their affliction and went on drinking and eating all the wrong things. Diabetics would drink, and fall into a coma. If a diabetic poetess was on a balcony looking at the moon—I swear to God, one of the detectives actually said that—she might fall over. The result would be the same, they said. Carver, I told them Olive wasn't like that; she didn't have any kind of death wish or fatal denial phobia."

"I don't remember reading anything about it."

"The story was buried in the middle of the *Chronicle* and the *Examiner*. Olive Dale was not a famous poet, but she had a wonderful kind of metaphysical humor toward life. But she wasn't important enough to rate a front-page story.'' Her voice fell to a whisper. ''Just another drunk who died from a fall. A fatal accident. Not important.''

She paused.

''How will I get it?'' she asked almost inaudibly. ''A fatal accident—or stabbed to death?''

SEVEN

''Royal, about Mr. Dale,'' Bea Murphy said. ''Didn't he say anything? He knew his wife took micronase.''

''He was in shock. But, yes, he tried to tell the police she didn't drink, but they figured he just didn't want the drunkenness stigma to be attached to his wife. Gordon is still in shock and mourning.''

Carver was silent. He'd check the newspaper back issues in the public library. And probably talk with Gordon Dale.

''Then,'' Royal Blue said, dragging out the word, giving it great significance, ''Geraldine Hare was killed. I had the terrible suspicion someone was killing poets. Female poets.''

''Any idea why?'' he asked.

''None at all, Carver.'' She looked at him, hoping to find a look in his face that would tell her he had a possible answer. ''It could be anything. Perhaps some jealous poet—or someone who has an obsession against lady poets. Oh, God, I'm scared!''

"Easy," Bea said, and put her arm around the younger woman.

"One thing I do know," Royal said, forcing herself to be firm, "it couldn't have been Laura who killed both of them."

"Why not?"

"Because she was across the bay in Oakland the night Olive Dale was pushed off her balcony. If she didn't kill Olive, then she didn't kill Geraldine."

"Sure, that doesn't necessarily follow," Bea said. "Laura could have another motive for killing Hare. And the Olive Dale death might have been an accident, as the police said. Or another person could have killed Olive Dale. Her husband, for instance." She drew herself straight under Royal Blue's stern gaze. "Don't jump on me, dear. I'm just playing devil's advocate. Those are just possibilities."

Carver wondered why the other poets in the group hadn't mentioned the death of Olive Dale to him. Why hadn't Laura? Lorna Stokes was certainly talkative enough. And Harold Yoshima seemed straightforward, didn't seem the sort to hold back pertinent information.

Carver made a mental note to speak with Yoshima again—after he had spoken to Laura De Anza. He had to know why she hadn't mentioned the death of Olive Beem Dale.

Royal put her toilet articles into the bathroom medicine chest. She turned and stood in the door between the bathroom and the living room. She smiled uneasily at him. Behind her the soft light framed her slender body, creating an ethereal glow around her.

Carver felt a familiar tug. Yeah, she was lovely. And smart. And creative. A combination that had always attracted him. In a pocket of his mind the lust and conquest syndrome awakened.

He put an arm around her shoulders. He felt Royal's body trembling. Yeah, she was uncertain. He slowly ran his hands over her tense back. She closed her eyes. He felt his own body responding to her closeness, her scent, her sensuality. Carver was in a tightening, familiar knot of sexual arousal.

Bea Murphy cleared her throat and opened the connecting door between the two rooms. She grinned at Carver.

64

"Not tonight, Henry," she quoted.

Carver compressed his lips and dropped his hands. He shook his head; forget it, he thought. And his head felt like broken glass and his ribs felt like a hot metal file had been scraped through them.

"In the morning," Royal said, "I'm going to have to phone my boss—"

"You'll have to call in sick," Carver said, notepad ready. "Where do you work?"

She gave him the name, address, and phone number of a computer company on Montgomery Street, where she worked as a processor. Her voice dropped.

"I'm real scared, Carver," she said, the words barely audible.

"You have a right to be," Bea said to her. "But you're not the only female poet in the group. There's Stokes and Kraft. And Laura, of course."

"Yeah," Carver said, "but she's had her door battered. And she's had a warning written in lipstick on her mirror."

"Yes, that's it," Royal admitted in the same distant voice. "I was already fearful before this happened—I'd talked with several of the poets in the group—"

"Who?" he asked.

She rattled off three names: Barbara Dwane, Susan Gerome, and Jack Bovee. The first two had not been at Hatt's, but Jack Bovee was. And Carver was going to talk with Bovee. Tomorrow.

And he'd talk with Sergeant Ernest Ludlow. He'd know who had been on the team that handled Olive Dale's death. Or maybe De Anza could tell him. Or the newspapers might have the information.

The lights burned late at the Hall of Justice on Bryant Street. In the Homicide Bureau, Lieutenant Raphael De Anza worked at his desk. A lean detective named Horta sidled over.

"Workin' late, huh, Lieutenant?"

"Yes, Dick. Working late."

65

"I guess you know how we all feel," Horta said. "It's a shame. But you know—"

"What?" De Anza asked, and looked at the detective. "What do I know, amigo?"

"Well, it's a bad scene. We heard rumors you got this nigger PI workin' for you. Now you know that looks bad for the bureau—not to say what it looks like to the whole force."

"It's my right."

"See, that's what I mean. With that 'rights' shit, you're soundin' like some kinda criminal, like you got somethin' to hide. Know what I mean?"

"Fuck off, Horta."

"Hey, Lieutenant, that ain't fair. You know it's not what I think. I was just giving you some of the stuff that's been goin' around. Hell, it don't bother me none that you hang around with nigger private cops and the faggot queers on the force. Well, shit, I ain't livin' in the backwoods, if you get my—"

"Horta! Fuck off!" Sergeant Ludlow said, as he stepped to De Anza's desk. "You heard the lieutenant. And if you didn't, you sure as hell heard me."

"Yeah, Sergeant, sure, I heard you."

Horta moved off, muttering under his breath, "You try to set a guy straight and look what you get, well, screw him, see . . ."

"If he makes sergeant," Ludlow said, settling into a chair, "I'll turn in my badge. Swear it."

"What can I do for you, Ernie?"

"Got you doin' desk work?"

"Yes. You know. They don't want me messing up the case against Laura. They want me where they can see me—to keep me off the streets where I might work on the Hare case. As I damn well would!"

"Don't worry about it. I don't believe she did it."

De Anza stared at him.

"You don't," he said. "Why didn't you tell me before?"

"I wanted to see things for myself. I've been out on my own time talkin' with those poets. There's somethin' there, and I don't like it. I've talked with this pizza-drivin' lady,

66

Stokes. She has an alibi. There's this other female, a hooker, Holliday Kraft—she's so slick I almost slid in pussy grease. She says a lot and says nothin'. Bascombe has already interrogated her. He told her about me, said I was mean and ugly. I told her he was a con artist, a wise ass.''

"Not good," De Anza said.

"So what? Anytime I can fuck over your buddy—anyway, I saw this other guy, this Jap guy, Yoshima. I don't like him at all. Too talkative, too glib. Bascombe told him I was comin', so I told Yoshima the black bastard was evil, real nosy, never let go of anything, and a blabbermouth to boot.''

"Ernie, you're ruffling feathers—including mine.''

"Look, Raf, if Laura didn't do it, then someone else did. That's logic. I'm talkin' to Captain Callahan and tell him what I've been doing. They can chain you to a desk, but not me. Me and Gulden will get permission to keep looking into this. Even though Callahan is another honky asshole, he respects my abilities. So it won't be long. I'm going to get Geraldine Hare's killer, and you'll owe me again.''

"Do that, and I won't mind if I owe you the store."

In the foyer of his house, Carver leaned against the heavy, wooden sliding doors. He activated the pocket recorder and made a note to warn Lorna Stokes and Holliday Kraft. If someone was killing lady poets, they had to be warned. Also he wanted to talk to Kraft about Lloyd.

Satisfactory. Even though his head ached and his ribs burned and he was tired to his bones.

"Carver?" a voice called from upstairs.

Claire Overton—he'd almost forgotten her. He trudged up the stairs, dragging his trench coat. God, he was dead.

She stood by the banister on the second floor. She rubbed sleep from her eyes, and the movement slid her sheer silken gown over her body. She seemed pleased to see him. She noticed Carver moved slowly, not his usual two-at-a-step climb up the stairs.

Claire put an arm around him, inquiring what had happened. He told her an abbreviated version, that two guys resented his investigation.

"But that's terrible, Carver," she said, and opened the door to his bedroom.

She helped him out of his coat. He sat on the edge of the rumpled, still-warm bed. Her favorite perfume hung in the air, as it had for almost a week. Joy. He was all right, he assured her; he'd live to fight another day.

"Is that all you think about?" Claire demanded. "Damn it, Carver, you're like a kid playing some kind of game in a playground. It's all such throwback romantic bullshit anyway. Honestly, you should be doing something more realistic. I can help you do that, you know."

"What?" he asked tiredly. He fell back onto the turned-down sheets. "What are you talking about?"

"Getting you a job—in television."

"Doing what, Claire?"

"The news," she said, a hint of exasperation showing. "Your talents and background as an investigator would fit right in with the news department. With a few years doing background research and investigative journalism under your belt, with that kind of experience, you could probably move out in front of the camera."

"Reading the news off a teleprompter?"

"The pay is fantastic."

"Yeah. I'd feel like an idiot," he said, and rubbed a hand over the warm, blue, percale sheets. "I'd probably wind up reading the weather—the token black weatherman."

He slipped off his shoes. Slowly he rubbed his feet together.

"I don't think you realize your own potential here."

"I just want to sleep."

"Okay, Carver," Claire said and sat next to him. "I do want to apologize for this morning. I woke up with the most horrendous headache—and I had to grin and bear it under the studio lights. Those hot things didn't help any."

Carver grunted, almost asleep. Claire gently stroked his face, touched her lips to his closed eyelids. She moved a hand down his chest, unbuttoning his shirt, then slowly rubbed below his belt.

"Anyway, I wanted to apologize," she said softly, "and to let you know I'll take care of things from now on. Okay?"

He rolled over, out, out, out.

EIGHT

"What time is it, Rose?"

"Jesus, you look terrible!"

Rose Weinbaum jumped from her desk and went to Carver Bascombe. He stood barefoot in the doorway, looking as if the only thing holding him upright were rumpled slacks and a dirty pullover shirt.

Rose helped him into his office. He plunked into his chair and rubbed his naked feet together.

"I gather you didn't do too well last night," Rose said.

"Rose—you gather right. You are one smart PI." He slid his mini-cassette recorder across his desk. "Transcribe that—"

"Please?"

"Yes, please, Rose."

"Will do, Boss. Anything you want to talk about? Like that lovely mess around your eye? You don't see that combination of colors every day. Very trendy. Very gross."

"Somebody wants me to stop investigating this case."

"Who'd want Laura on ice, Carver?"

"I don't think it's that. Her arrest was just a bonus for someone. No, it's something else."

"Explain, please?"

"Since Laura didn't kill Geraldine Hare—and that's a given—then someone else had a motive for killing Hare. The killer wasn't trying to lay the blame on Laura—he or she is taking advantage of the cops' bullheadedness."

"So you haven't found anyone who saw Laura on her walk?"

"Not yet. Has Tettsui called in?"

"No. Neither has Murphy. I'll get on this tape transcription."

In a few moments she had on her headset and was typing up the events on the tape. Carver relaxed and went to the sideboard. Rose had coffee in the usual vacuum jug, and he praised her silently. He poured himself a cup of coffee.

He returned to his desk and doodled on a pad. Laura. Lorna Stokes. Holliday Kraft. Yoshima. Blue—Royal Blue. A beautiful woman. A lovely, frightened woman.

Royal had that special something that appealed to Carver. Beauty and artistic talent. And intelligence. A combination he rarely resisted. She was a woman who knew what she wanted.

Royal Blue exuded a sensuality—a sexuality mixed with art. Her inner self was revealed by her poetry, her art—as the other poets would with their poems.

He hadn't talked to Jack Bovee as yet. He sketched little arrows between the group of names on the notepad, linking them all. He'd talk with Laura De Anza again. Bring her up to date. Then he'd see Jack Bovee.

He drank more coffee, trying to dislodge something that nagged at his mind. It tugged at a gray area he couldn't quite see. His inner eye was out of order. What was bugging him?

Not the beating by the two white guys. He was sure he knew who had sent them. Lloyd the pimp, via Holliday Kraft. For some reason she thought he might make trouble for her. Or bring the spotlight of the law on her. Which would happen anyway, whether Carver talked to her or not.

Lloyd without-a-last-name had sent the two guys. Butt out, Bascombe.

Like hell! Carver thought.

No, something else bothered him, and it was something recent. Last night? Something someone had told him? Something he'd seen?

He went over the events, clicking them off automatically in his mind. They flowed through and none of the interviews with Stokes or Kraft or Yoshima or Royal revealed anything. And his memory was usually damn good.

He'd wait and read the transcribed pages from the cassette tape.

He called the motel and spoke with Bea Murphy. Everything was okay. Carver promised to drop by later. Yeah—he wanted to see Royal Blue again. He felt himself sexually aroused just thinking of her.

Then he called Lorna Stokes at the Par-Cheesey shop, but it wasn't open as yet. He'd call later. Next he called Holliday Kraft. She answered on the tenth ring.

"Yes?" she said, the word somehow sexually inviting.

He identified himself and told her to be careful. She wanted to know why.

"Someone might be killing the female poets in the group," he said. "Geraldine Hare might have been the second victim."

"What kind of a crazy thing is that to tell a lady before nine in the morning. That big black cop, he told me about you! So why should I believe you?"

"That's up to you, Holliday. You might want to tell Lloyd. Get those two goons to keep an eye on you."

"What goons? You're not making any sense—"

Carver hung up. Then he scribbled the name Olive Beem Dale on a notepad and handed it to Rose.

"So?" she asked. "Who's this?"

"She's a poet, as you'll hear on the tape. Check her out at the public library. Cross-reference as much stuff on her as you can find."

Claire Overton swept in, made up, wearing a fine suit, skirt, and jacket in apricot tones, with a honey-colored silk blouse. A lavender scarf tied rakishly askew over her shoulder gave her a debonair, carefree appearance. She paused at Rose Weinbaum's desk.

71

"Good morning, Rose," Claire said pleasantly. She turned to Carver. "And you, too, Carver. How are you feeling?"

"I'll live, Claire," he said.

"God, I'm glad. You had a terrible night."

She came to him and planted a kiss on his forehead. It felt almost patronizing.

"That'll help you feel better," she said.

Rose asked if Claire wanted coffee.

"No, honey," she answered, her eyes on Carver. "I don't need it. I'm jacked up enough already."

"Really?" Rose said.

"Oh, just a little idea of something for my show this morning," Claire said, and turned her smile to Carver. "You ought to watch my program today, lover."

"If I get a chance, Claire," he said.

"If I keep this up, I might get a network show. I know I can outdo Oprah. She'd never have a chance against me. Good looks count for a lot. Even in the news department." She turned to Rose. "I'm sorry about the scene yesterday. Sometimes I think the curse is so well named. Anyway, it makes me such a bitch. I'll be back after lunch—after my show."

Carver rubbed his stubbly chin. How was he going to let her down? he asked himself. He couldn't keep her around during this case.

"What are you thinking about, lover?"

Carver shook his head.

NINE

"Why don't you shower and scrape your face," Claire said, "and I'll wait for you. I don't have to be at the studio until ten. We could have breakfast at that place over on Stanyan, the little bed-and-breakfast place?"

Carver nodded and trudged upstairs. Maybe Jimmy Bowman was right; maybe he did have a concussion. He promised himself to take it easier for the rest of the day.

Somewhere, down deep, perhaps in Carver's mind, there was a derisive chuckle.

In the steaming shower, he slowly rubbed soap all over—and then let teeth-chattering, bone-chilling icy water spray over him. After shaving he toweled roughly and went naked into his walk-in closet.

Half-a-dozen Brioni suits enticed him. He chose a gray one, with faint dark blue pinstripes. The lining was blue silk, patterned with a modern, muted paisley design. He eyed his fifty or so shirts, which were neatly laid out on a series of shelves. Pale cream, Carver decided, and a fine silk tie of the same material as the coat lining.

He felt a hell of a lot better.

As he decided which pair of handmade shoes to wear, he remembered the shoes he wore last night. Carver picked them up. Bits of mirror glass from Royal Blue's apartment were still imbedded in the soles. Yes, he thought, as he remembered the other piece of glass he had pried out.

Was it important? Some kind of message was trying to get through his aching head. What was it?

One thing for sure, he had to get his mind off Claire Overton. He was impatient to see Laura De Anza once more and to talk with the last poet on his list: Jack Bovee. He'd postpone breakfast with Claire.

Something in his mind went *click*. Carver remembered about the piece of glass embedded in his shoe. He had picked it up in Lorna Stokes's car. And the shape of it—curved and coated inside with dark soot. The glass was from a cocaine free base pipe. Probably Stokes was a crack user.

Very bad shit. But none of his business. Not yet at any rate.

He stuffed his torn suit into a plastic bag, tossed his trench coat over one arm, and went downstairs. Rose and Claire were enjoying cigarettes together, and Claire had apparently been bending Rose's ear with TV behind-the-scenes anecdotes.

"I'm almost finished, boss," Rose said, indicating the transcription earphones. "I got past the interesting part—" She stressed the word *interesting*.

Carver asked Claire to step outside; he needed to talk to Rose privately. Claire walked out. Ungraciously.

"What's up, boss. The research—I'll drive to the library, get an early start."

"In addition to Kraft and Dale, I'm interested in Lorna Stokes. I suspect she's a cocaine user—"

"Crack?"

"Yeah. And I want you to buy all the books of poems by all the poets that were at Hatt's. Try City Lights. They should have more than I have in my library. Particularly Jack Bovee. I only have his stuff in an anthology."

"You want it in the next three minutes? Or can I do it after I'm through typing? On my old-fashioned electric typewriter?"

"You're still hinting for a computer."

"I am. We need one."

"When you've got something, call me at De Anza's."

He went into the hallway and apologized to Claire Overton.

74

"Sorry, Claire. I've got to postpone breakfast—but I'll make it up to you."

"Well, I don't know," she said, making a show of being mildly irritated. "But if you're really that busy—then that later has to be a promise."

Ten minutes later Carver pulled to the curb at the TV station. Claire climbed out, in a good mood, and gaily entered the lobby. Carver dropped his torn suit off at Wilkes Bashford's for repairs, then headed toward the Mission District. He parked in front of the De Anza home. Laura opened the door.

"I was expecting you," she said, and hugged him, and asked him inside.

Laura De Anza was a lovely woman. But she was frightened and tired. Her pulled-back graying hair seemed more severe than usual. She ran a hand nervously over her high, Aztec-inherited cheeks. She looked older, with her wide almond eyes moist and red-rimmed. The skin around her nose was pinched.

Laura didn't look as if she could hold on much more. She needed counseling. Raphael and their son, Antonio, could only be of so much help and support. As they sat in the living room, Laura lowered the sound on the TV.

"Have you found anyone?" she asked.

"Not yet."

Carver brought her up to date. The two PI's had found no one. The information was not comforting. He did not tell her about the two men who beat him up, nor about the broken door to Royal's apartment.

"Geraldine's funeral is day after tomorrow," Laura said. "I want to attend, but Raphael says it would not be wise."

"I think he's right. I'll try to attend."

The phone rang and Laura answered it; it was Rose Weinbaum for Carver.

"Go ahead, Rose," he said, and held the recorder to the receiver.

"Boss, I found Olive Dale's story in the newspaper back issues. I've had them dry-copied for our files. You'll want them—anyway, the news information on Olive Dale's death jells with Royal Blue's story. Olive Dale, a housewife—not even a poet for God's sake—had fallen—accidental, the cops said—to her death—two Fridays ago.''

"Thanks, Rose.''

"There's a lot more in the poetry magazines, so I'd better stick with it here. Still looking for anything on Lorna Stokes. And then I'll buy those books.''

"You're doing great, Rose,'' he said, and hung up.

He put the recorder in his shirt pocket and returned to Laura De Anza. She asked if he'd like a beer. He said yes, and she went off to the kitchen. He looked out the living-room windows. The rain fell softly against the panes. The television softly muttered in the background.

Carver turned and looked and saw that it was the co-anchor on Claire Overton's morning chatty news and interview show. Laura returned with two bottles of Anchor Steam beer and glasses. She poured, and Carver took several appreciative sips.

"Laura,'' he began, "what do you know of Olive Dale?''

"Who?''

Carver explained who the poet had been, but not the circumstances of her death two Fridays before.

"I never knew her,'' Laura replied. "Why do you ask?''

Her puzzled expression was genuine. It was obvious she'd never met Olive Dale.

Without revealing the source, Carver retold the events as described by Royal Blue and the news clipping.

"Unbelievable,'' Laura said, her eyes excited. "But it is true, two Fridays ago I was in Oakland—but I must tell you, Carver, I came home before ten o'clock. I had a minor migraine, if such things can be considered minor.''

Olive Beem Dale had fallen (or been pushed) from her balcony after ten o'clock. Laura was not off the hook.

Behind him he heard his name mentioned. *Carver*. He turned and stared at the television set. Claire Overton was on-screen, giving her usual sincere look.

What was she saying? He turned up the volume control.

"The investigation into the murder of famed poetess Geraldine Hare has taken this new turn. Fortunately the assault on the private investigator was not fatal. Serious, but not deadly . . . not yet!

"But who paid for the beating of Carver Bascombe?—whom you may recall I interviewed only a few weeks ago—and why has he been warned off the De Anza case? Is this some kind of cover-up from City Hall? Or perhaps from the police department itself?

"Apparently the DA is unaware that several detectives do not believe that Laura De Anza is guilty of murder. Certainly not Lieutenant De Anza, who has hired the same Carver Bascombe to investigate the case. Or has he hired Bascombe to investigate the police?

"There will be more on this, so watch this time slot, because you'll get it here first."

"Goddamn it!" Carver cursed.

His thoughts raced. Claire had gravely compromised Carver's hunt for Laura De Anza's alibi.

Where had Claire found out her information? *When* had she found it? *How!* His mind reeled with the questions.

He stood rigid before the TV set. His hands clenched at his side, glaring at the vivid colors on the screen.

TEN

Carver slammed open his front door and raced upstairs. Damn! That's what his subconscious had been trying to tell him! The cassette tape! Rose at the typewriter—she hadn't rewound the microtape. She didn't have to. It had already been rewound. And except to hear his own mugging, Carver had not fully rewound it.

But someone had!

In Claire's dressing room, Carver grabbed one of her suitcases and flipped open the lid. He ran his hands expertly between the layers of clothing. Nothing there.

On a table, her portable double-cassette deck caught his eye. He snatched it up. Empty. No tapes in it.

He scanned the edge of the machine. Jack holes. Yeah, could be. In another suitcase he found a variety of cables with connecting jacks.

"Goddamn it," he cursed. Just what kind of games was Claire playing? Goddamn her!

He jammed a particular set of cables into his pocket. Then he tore open drawer after drawer and dumped all of Claire's clothes onto the floor. From the closets he gathered armfuls of dresses and sweaters and jackets and hurled them onto the floor.

Bitter, jerky movements. Into a large bag he emptied her jewelry and vanity bottles, lipsticks, mascara, eye shadow, body lotions, activator bottles, and shampoo and conditioner.

He shoved all the clothes into Claire's designer-label suitcases. He manhandled them to the top of the staircase and pitched them down, one after the other.

Cursing under his breath, he carried her cassette recorder and walked downstairs, his steps measured. He kicked his way through the jumble of luggage on the ground floor.

In his office he poured himself several ounces of Wild Turkey and tossed it back. He tossed his trench coat onto a chair. He told himself to calm down. Don't fly off! He forced himself to breathe deeply; long, measured breaths. Calm—goddamn it—calm.

He chose a tape of Mozart's *Linz Symphony* and listened to the ethereal, soothing music. He looked at his watch. Past one o'clock. He'd wait. Oh, yes, goddamn it, he'd wait.

On the stairs, Carver placed Claire Overton's player/recorder beside him. He drank the smooth bourbon.

Get his angry thoughts off Claire and her actions. He forced his mind to go over the paths of the past day. What did he have? From the beginning . . . A murder. The victim, Geraldine Hare. What had he learned about her?

He didn't think her lesbianism had much to do with her death—but he would keep an open mind about that.

Hare had been a temperamental, volatile poet—who had run afoul of Lorna Stokes and Laura De Anza, both also volatile personalities. Although Laura, to her credit, was not temperamental. Or if she was, she covered it well.

According to Royal Blue, Hare's murder was the second. Olive Beem Dale had been number one. According to Royal. Was some psycho after female poets? Would it take the death of a third female poet to wake up the police? Was Royal to be victim number three?

He cursed Claire again. The woman didn't have the brains to think far ahead. She was only after a story, didn't give a damn about the consequences!

Soon the media would descend. More ammunition for his neighbors. A few of them would like nothing better than to get rid of a black private detective that lived in their middle-class midst. Nothing but trouble for the neighborhood. Get rid of him! Buy him out!

Mozart did little to calm Carver.

He tried once again to force his mind to take paths of contemplation—but the squeal of brakes outside grabbed his attention.

He peeked out the front door. Several cars and a TV van had parked askew, and several reporters and camerapersons converged through the heavy drizzle.

Carver stepped out of eyesight of the front-door glass.

The doorbell rang. And rang. Loud voices hailed from outside.

"We know you're in there, Bascombe! Come on out!"

"What's the police department said to you?"

"One interview! Give us five minutes! And we'll leave you alone!"

Could they see the jumbled pile of luggage?

"Izzat right? That cop De Anza hired you?"

"Yeahyeah! He don't trust his own people or something?"

And more of that sort of thing. More, much more.

Carver was sick of the whole thing.

He waited—fearing that the telephone would ring—that De Anza would be on the line. What could Carver say? As usual he'd say little. Never complain, never explain. He'd deal with Claire Overton.

He heard a rattle from the kitchen. The bastards were trying to get in from the back!

Carver went into the kitchen.

Claire Overton was there, just shutting the rear door. She shook her umbrella, then turned and looked defiantly at him.

"I saw them from my taxi," she said. "I had the driver take me around the block."

"An explanation," Carver demanded.

"None necessary," Claire said, and brushed past him. In the hallway she stopped and stared at the jumbled pile of suitcases. She picked up one suitcase and glared at Carver. Her eyes seemed to rupture with fire.

"Have you lost your mind?!" she screamed.

"Shut up," he ordered.

He held out the cassette-deck recorder.

"You used this," he said. "You took my cassette from my pocket—and copied it."

"What? Are you crazy?" She grabbed the deck from his hands. Her face was bright with anger. "They're not even the same size cassettes."

"You used these." He removed the set of cables from his pocket. "Different-sized jacks on each end. It was easy."

She stared at him, her face at first twisted in fury—then subsided into a sardonic smile.

"All right, Carver—so what? I need good stories for my show. What did you expect? You were kicking me out of your life—"

"No—"

"Oh, yes! I know the signs. I've been around, too, you know! I can smell a brush-off when the wind is right."

Carver shook his head.

"Oh, yes, oh, yes!" Claire said. "You're fooling yourself. I was history!"

"You've fouled this investigation, Claire—"

"So?"

"You've probably devastated a friendship between me and Raphael De Anza—"

"Yes, well, big deal. A cop!"

"But worst—worst of all, Claire," he said, his words flat, hard, the syllables bitten down, "—you just might've put an innocent woman in prison. Maybe death row."

"The cop's wife? You really believe she's innocent? What the hell, Carver, are you naive? I've heard the scam on her, what the cops have got—and it's plenty! The only reason, the *only* reason, she's out on bail is she's the wife of a homicide detective. And to me, that kind of preferential treatment smells—not only of favoritism, but corruption. And it's my duty, my job, and my pleasure—*my pleasure!*—to bring it to the attention of the public!"

ELEVEN

Carver held out his hand.

"Keys."

Claire glared at him—then rummaged in her purse and

handed him a key ring. She cursed him, then demanded the phone.

"To call a cab!"

Again Carver sat on the stairs and waited. Claire stood near the front door. Neither spoke. About fifteen minutes later a taxi pulled up and the driver made his way through the waiting reporters.

Claire opened the door and she and the taxi driver hauled her suitcases to the taxi. Carver closed the door. Claire waved gaily to the camerawoman from a rival TV station. She fielded their questions with practiced ease, and a few minutes later Claire was gone.

Carver looked at his watch; he had work to do. He tossed the keys Claire had given him into his desk drawer. He put fresh batteries and a mini-cassette into the recorder.

He put in a call to Bea Murphy, who had nothing to report; everything at her end seemed normal. Royal Blue was typing, and the rain was still coming down.

Carver spent a few minutes rubbing his feet. He changed the music from Mozart to Ibert's *Ports of Call*, preferring the less mathematical piece. From his desk he took Rose's transcript pages and pinned them to a corkboard.

He telephoned Jack Bovee. After a dozen rings he was about to hang up when it was answered.

"Yes?" a voice asked.

"Jack Bovee?" Carver asked.

"Uh . . . yes, I'm Bovee. Who is this?"

"My name is Carver Bascombe—"

"Oh, sure!" Bovee said, changing his tone, less cautious, friendlier. "You're the private detective. Yosh told me you probably wanted to talk to me."

Carver admitted he did and asked for a convenient time to come over.

"I've been out for a while," Bovee said, "but I'm going to be here most of the day. My place isn't much, but then I don't need much. My wants are small. My poetry makes me rich."

Carver said he'd be over in a while and hung up. He went

to the corkboard and studied the transcripts pinned there. Let his thoughts roam.

Then he heard another commotion, and he looked out the front-window drapes. Rose Weinbaum had driven into the driveway next to the house. She got out, flailed her umbrella at the reporters, and entered the front door. She carried a bundle of packages.

She removed her damp scarf and looked at Carver.

"I heard about the TV show," she said, putting her packages on her desk.

Carver nodded and said nothing.

"Oh, I know how you feel," she said. She sat at her desk and lit a cigarette. "Something like that happened with Bernie and me once. I couldn't understand why Bernie was so outraged. After all, it's not as if he hadn't pulled some neat tricks of his own on other people. I figured it was how you looked at it—whose ox is being gored."

Carver shrugged.

"Blue okay?" Rose asked.

Carver nodded.

"Ah, the Bascombe silence. The Gary Cooper of private eyes. Strong and silent. Or are you just embarrassed? Come on, talk to me. Where'd you put her?"

"Nedden's," he said.

"Oh, good. Murphy still with her, of course." She blew smoke over her typewriter. "Now what? You still have at least one more guy to talk to—Jack Bovee. I bought a bunch of little books of his poetry. And everyone else's, too. Cost a bunch."

He was silent. He went to the bar and poured another Wild Turkey. He sipped the bourbon. The smell of the alcohol mingled with the odor of tobacco. He rubbed one stockinged foot against the other, and Ibert's music sailed on to another island.

"Okay, be like that," Rose said. "I spent a few moments talking with people at the telephone company. Remarkable how much information Information has. I got Gordon Dale's office and home address and phone numbers. He's a fairly well-known architect in the Bay Area. I called his office, but

Dale won't talk with anyone about his wife's death. 'Her fall,' he said. So—now what, Boss? Tell the cops?''

"No," Carver said finally. "Not yet, anyway."

"Ah. Close to the vest."

"See what you can do about getting me an appointment with Gordon Dale."

Rose tilted her head, then picked up the phone. She used her sexy voice to convince Olive Dale's husband he had to see Mr. Bascombe.

"... he's a most discreet person, Mr. Dale. If you're concerned, I can give you some excellent references to Mr. Bascombe's character and abilities. . . ."

She gave him several names, including LeRoy Dolny's, Carver's friend who owned an art gallery.

"All right, Miss Weinbaum—I'll give your employer ten minutes. Today. Say one o'clock?"

"That would be fine, Mr. Dale. Mr. Bascombe will see you. And thank you—you're most generous."

Dale grunted and hung up.

"You're set, Boss," Rose said to Carver. "What's the plan for today?"

"I've got to talk with—with Harold Yoshima and Holliday Kraft. And Jack Bovee. The last player."

"You're not talking with any of the other poets?"

"No." He drank more of the Wild Turkey. "If that doesn't get me somewhere, I'll start from square one."

"Yes, Carver," Rose said gently, "that might be necessary. Start over with Lorna Stokes and Holliday Kraft and Harold Yoshima."

"Yeah. I've warned Kraft, and I'll get to Stokes. The women in the group—Laura, Blue—they might be in danger—"

"You don't sound too convinced."

"No. There's something going on. But I can't put my hand on it. My thoughts are spinning, trying to tell me something. I've heard or seen something that doesn't quite fit."

"The hunter hunts," Rose said. "We've seen something like this before. Your subconscious is usually right."

He thumbed through the books Rose had purchased. He

84

selected several volumes on Harold Yoshima and read silently.

> *Son, who made the condition*
> *smooth words like old jugged syrup*
> *to ooze over the jagged reflection*
> *of all too dull to see the ruse . . .*

And later:

> *Harrow, the harlequin, masked to eye*
> *garment to clothe, not as it was*
> *but echoed as through tilted glass*
> *not as it was, but as jubilee guile . . .*

After several pages he put aside the volume and read some of the works of Jack Bovee. Then Holliday Kraft. The long minutes were shaded by the clacking of Rose's typewriter. Finally Carver closed the volume he was reading. Rose stopped typing and looked at him.

"So?" she said.

"So I need more information on Yoshima, Bovee, Kraft, Stokes, and—" He paused. "And Royal Blue. As much as you can find out."

"In-depth background? Financial? Social? Above and beyond statistics?"

"Yeah." He tossed back the last swallow of bourbon. His thoughts were dark, brooding. "All that. One thing we might try—Yoshima said he worked at a computer firm—East Wind Process in Silicon Valley. Contact Herb Randall—"

"At Tan-ta-Mount Logic?"

Carver nodded. He had installed the electonic security system in Randall's computer-software-company plant and headquarters in Silicon Valley. Randall had been more than pleased. He was a black man who believed in helping others—especially black men and women. Three-quarters of his employees were black.

"I'll get right on it, Boss."

Carver laced his fingers together and slowly wrenched them.

"Damn Claire," he said.

His words were soft—soft, and regretful.

TWELVE

"Want it filled up, Cahvah?" Jimmy Bowman asked.

Carver nodded. He sat in the Chrysler, staring out the windshield. He had a lot to ponder. (He forced Claire from his thoughts; he couldn't afford the anger.)

Jimmy Bowman unscrewed the cap and shoved in the gas nozzle.

"Want the windows cleaned?" he asked.

Carver shook his head. What was Raphael De Anza going to think about this three-ring circus? What would Ludlow think? Carver didn't like any of the possibilities. The whole damn case was about to get flushed down the toilet.

"I been thinkin'," Jimmy said.

"Yeah?"

"About your other car. The fancy blue Jag. Now that's a machine that's more your style, Cahvah. The way I figger it, you owe a bundle to a bank—or you'd be drivin' that fine machine around. So—"

"Yeah, so?"

"Now I got me a lot of money sittin' in a bank, not doin' much of nothin'. What it is, you oughtta be drivin' that car.

It's your style, know what I mean? I'd like to help you get it off them blocks in your garage—''

"No, Jimmy," Carver said.

"Come on, man! You helped me plenty in the past."

"You've helped me, too. No, thanks, Jimmy, but I can't take your offer. But thanks."

"Can't say I didn' try. Put the gas on your bill?"

Carver nodded and about fifteen minutes later he was parked three blocks from Harold Yoshima's apartment, the closest space he could find.

Yoshima was opening his garage when Carver strode up.

"Mr. Bascombe," Yoshima said, as he recognized the private detective. "What brings you back?"

"Just a few questions."

"Well, Mr. Bascombe, let's not stand in the rain. I'm sure we are intelligent enough to know when to get out of the rain. Come—there's a small coffee shop in North Beach where I often go."

Carver said that was fine, and he and Yoshima drove the few blocks to Columbus Avenue. Yoshima parked and they went into a Italian café. Yoshima ordered a sweet roll and café au lait, and Carver ordered coffee.

"Now, Mr. Bascombe, what is it you wish to know?"

"About Royal Blue. She was your dinner guest."

"Yes, she was. I gather you've talked with her?"

"Not about her visiting you."

The waiter brought the roll and coffees. Yoshima smiled and admired the quality of the pastry. Carver drank his heavy-flavored coffee, then held the cup between his hands, warming them.

"Aah," Yoshima said, smacking his lips. "About Miss Blue—I've almost finished with the dummy mock-up of the anthology. I like the idea of publishing. There are many small presses in the Bay Area, and I thought I might try my hand at it. I have no interest in butting heads with the big New York publishing empires."

"You'd like to do something artistic?"

"That is it precisely." He bit into the roll and rolled his eyes. He made pleasure sounds, then continued. "I wanted to see if Miss Blue would be interested in having an edition of her poems printed. A very quality printing to be sure. Illustrated with very classic artwork. I think I could sell five thousand copies—with decent distribution.''

"Now about Olive Beem Dale?''

"You do know how to jump to a new subject. Olive Dale . . . a most tragic life. Married to . . . I'm sorry, but I'm not a gossip.''

"Did you tell the police about her?''

"No. Why should I?'' he mused, stroking his tie. "Her death had nothing to do with the poetry group. The police never asked me anything at the time. Since then, of course, I've spoken to them, including the man you warned me about—Sergeant Ludlow. A most unpleasant fellow.''

"Tell me about Dale. Anything.''

"I think you are a most persistent person. And you probably already know much. You are probably comparing what you know with my statements. So—can you take direct talk? Of course you can. You are a very blunt person.''

"Yeah,'' Carver said. "Go on.''

"Olive Dale was an excellent poet. Her poems were filled with angst. Probably because of her sexual proclivities.''

"Meaning what?''

"She was a lesbian, Mr. Bascombe.''

"She was married.''

Harold Yoshima shrugged eloquently.

"To be sure. I assume it was a smoke screen. Her husband is homosexual. Theirs was a—how shall I say it? A marriage of convenience.''

A hunch unfolded in Carver's mind. He thought he'd try it out on Yoshima—and watch the man's reaction.

"Olive Dale had a lesbian lover—and this lover was also Geraldine Hare's lover.''

"You are most quick-witted, Mr. Bascombe.''

"Do you know who she was?''

Yoshima shook his head.

"Any rumors? Had you ever heard that this lover might be Holliday Kraft?''

"No, I've never heard such a thing.''

"All right. Now, about Jack Bovee—"

"A most interesting fellow. A fine workingman's poet. A good coeditor—although we often argue. I've told him about you. He's fascinated and is looking forward to meeting you."

Carver did not reveal he had a meeting with Bovee later. He did not expound on the possibility of the female poets being in danger. They finished their coffee.

"Well, I must go," Yoshima said. "I am taking a few days off from work to finish the anthology—and to make myself available to the police. I don't relish having my employer annoyed by visits from the police."

They shook hands, and Carver trudged up the hill to where he had parked his car.

THIRTEEN

The downtown parking attendant hopped into Carver's Chrysler and drove it off into the gloom and damp of the underground garage. Carver took the elevator to the twentieth floor, where Gordon Dale had his architectural offices.

Dale's secretary admitted Carver immediately. Dale's office was pristine and modern, airy and light-filled, with a cream lacquered desk. The rest of the furniture matched, in golds and glass and pastel colors.

Dale was a large man, muscular, with big hands that rested flat on his desk. Carver figured he looked like an anxious bodybuilder, as though lifting weights and working out would reverse middle age creeping up on him.

There was another person in the office: a woman with blond hair cut short and wearing an executive-style skirt, blouse, and jacket. A lavender scarf was the one colorful accessory.

"Mr. Bascombe," Dale said, the words fast and blunt. "Let's get to it, shall we."

Carver nodded. He wondered what the hurry was.

"First, let's get some things straight. I did check the references your secretary gave me. I was only impressed with one—from LeRoy Dolny. You'll know why in a minute—"

"Because you're gay," Carver said. "And LeRoy said you could trust me."

"Right! And LeRoy said to be open with you, that you were a man to be trusted. I trust LeRoy implicitly. Okay—" He turned to the woman. "This is JoAnne Stanton—"

Introductions went around. Dale paced the office while JoAnne Stanton picked up the conversation. Her voice was brisk, businesslike. She had a habit of running her hands through her pageboy-cut honey-blond hair.

"Time is money," Stanton said, "and Gordon has an important meeting with the architectural commission in less than an hour. So, as he said, let's get to it, and put our cards on the table."

Carver nodded, already guessing what was ahead. JoAnne Stanton drew a deep breath, her breasts swelling.

"The police will soon be looking into our affairs. We can't stop that, but we hope we can sidetrack any potential scandal which might ruin Gordon's business. Do you follow me so far?"

Carver said he did.

"Good!" she said. "I don't look like it, I suppose, but I'm in deep mourning—"

"For Geraldine Hare," Carver guessed.

"Yes, for Geraldine. I was her lover, Mr. Bascombe." She rubbed her hands together and looked at Gordon Dale, who gestured encouragingly for her to continue. "And—and I was also Olive Dale's lover."

"I guessed," Carver lied calmly.

"Then you are quite shrewd." JoAnne Stanton looked with admiration at Gordon Dale. "Gordon is a dear man. He shared his life with Olive and me, and we all lived quite comfortably because of him. However—"

"However," Gordon Dale said, picking up the narration, "there is the possibility—no, the probability—that the police are going to perceive the two deaths as somehow related. That someone, perhaps a cast-off lover, such as JoAnne, might have killed them both in a jealous rage. I assure you, there was no jealousy. Our affairs, between ourselves, were quite open."

"Why tell me?" Carver asked.

"Because we might need your services. To protect us, to help us avoid a scandal—and if possible to point the finger at the true murderer of Geraldine and my wife."

"I'm sorry," Carver said, shaking his head, "but I have a client."

"Well, then—I assume you mean Laura De Anza is your client. You see, we watch the Overton program, too—"

"I assume you don't think Laura is guilty."

"Correct, Mr. Bascombe. I've met Laura several times, but as temperamental as she is, she doesn't have it in her to kill someone. However—I might have that quality."

"So, Mr. Bascombe," Dale said, "when you have completed that job, then you might consider our offer. I can be quite generous to a discreet investigator."

Carver said he'd keep the offer in mind.

They talked some more, with Carver getting answers that matched most of the others he had been getting. Gordon Dale said he did not know any of the other poets—except for Geraldine Hare—since his wife had never officially joined the poetry group. As for Geraldine Hare, Gordon knew her because of his friendship with JoAnne Stanton.

Carver thanked them and left. Outside, he turned off the recorder in his shirt pocket. Rose Weinbaum would certainly notice the information on this tape, he thought.

91

FOURTEEN

Carver pulled into Nedden's motel on Lombard Street. Bea Murphy let him in.

"Everything okay?" he asked as he pulled off his wet trench coat.

"Yes, of course," Murphy replied. "What did you expect, lad? That some crazed killer has gained a cosmic sense of ESP and tracked the lovely Miss Blue to this motel? Not bloody likely, I'll tell you."

"No, just concerned."

"You've heard nothing from Mike Tettsui then?"

"Not a peep."

"No news is good news, Carver."

"You really know how to sound original, Bea."

"I've been having a good think while I rested up here—on salary of course—and I've decided you can call me Murph."

"Why?"

"Because Bea sounds like a plump honey-making insect. And I've always hated the name—"

"We could call you Beatrice—"

"Bloody hell!" Murphy said. "Not likely that. Bea is bad enough."

Carver grinned and knocked on the connecting door. Royal Blue called for him to come in.

"I heard you talking to Bea," Royal said as Carver stepped into her room. "You have a very distinctive voice."

"Do I?"

"Yes, as I'm sure you're well aware. Not a baritone, but not a tenor either, just sort of gruff and powerful. Am I embarrassing you?"

Carver shrugged. A fraudulent shrug; he wanted her to continue talking.

"I've been thinking a lot," she said, "about all this. I don't want to see Laura go to prison. Or to the gas chamber. And I've been thinking about living. How precious it is. And I've been thinking about Geraldine Hare. About her funeral. It's tomorrow, isn't it?

He nodded, saying nothing, watching her.

"And I've thought about you," she said. "You seem to be a man who likes to help people. I don't know your reasons for that—but I would like to find out."

"It's a case of enriched curiosity," he said. "I like to know why people do things. For instance—why did Yoshima invite you to dinner last night?"

"He's a friend, Carver. But how did you know I was there? Really?"

"Your perfume—Patou one thousand. I wondered how you could afford it."

"I got it in Paris five years ago. I have very little of it left."

"Yoshima must've had a specific reason to invite you."

"Yes, he wanted to see if I was interested in having my poems brought out in a special edition. He would like very much to get into the publishing business. In a small way, of course, he said."

"And?"

"Well, to put it bluntly, publishing is risky. Particularly in the small-press business. It would help, he said, if he had a few books that would be guaranteed to sell. He wanted to know if I'd be interested if he published a special edition of my erotic poems—with illustrations from classic Japanese erotic artists."

"What did you say?"

"I told him I was flattered, and that I'd think about it. That's one reason I was walking around in the rain afterward. Much the same as you were doing. Walking in the rain. In that way we have similar likes."

"Yes," he said.

"I thought we might get along. I think our souls would blend."

Carver's body responded before his mind caught her nuances. He felt strong, hard, sexual. Was she aware of the effect she had on him? He reached out and touched her hand.

She felt cool, yet tense. The tendons in her fingers were tight, and her hand trembled. He looked into her eyes, moist and earth-brown like a harvest field freshly rained upon.

He recited several lines from her controversial poem.

"Open the envelope, feel the check
it's not the same as his, not like his—"

"I've written other poems," Royal Blue said and smiled.

"I like it—because it's implicit."

"It's not about sex and orgasms as a metaphor for equal rights. It's the other way around. It's about equal rights, using the orgasm as a metaphor."

He held her gently around the shoulders, his face close to her. She gazed at him, her eyes open, unblinking. He felt her breathing, deep and strong.

"Emily Dickinson once said about poetry," Blue said, " 'If I feel physically as if the top of my head were taken off, I know that is poetry.' "

"Interesting," Carver said softly.

He drew her closer. Blue's breathing was quick and heavy. Her body felt full, ready to burst.

"I feel that way about love and sex," she said. "An orgasm can be like that. Pure poetry. When I feel the top of my head going off, I know sex is poetry."

Her lips opened under his mouth, and they stood together for long moments. Carver Bascombe had never felt so powerful, so saturated with life. He knew she also felt it.

She reached up and held his face in her hands. She leaned back and looked at him. She licked her lips.

"Carver . . ." she said softly.

"Later, Royal, later. There's time."

She shuddered and pressed herself against him. They kissed again, her hands gently exploring Carver's shoulders. She felt totally comfortable in his embrace. Her mind settled gently in a warm flood, without fear, without pain. She felt aroused and lightly floating.

Then the beeper at his waist went off.

"Damn it," Blue said hoarsely.

FIFTEEN

Royal grabbed herself in an angry hug. She glared at the beeper, which still emitted its squealing sound.

Carver thumbed it off and went to the phone. He got the number from his paging service and called Tettsui.

"Carver, I got him," Tettsui said. "Laura's alibi. A guy saw her that night—remembers her well."

"I'm on my way. Where are you?"

"At this guy's shop," Tettsui said and gave the address, which was on the northern slope of Nob Hill.

Carver said he'd be there in less than ten minutes.

"I remember her well," Clyde Netsuke said slowly.

"Why?" Carver asked.

Carver and Tettsui were in Clyde Netsuke's small objet d'art shop, which contained curios and carvings and fabrics from far-off places like Burma, the Philippines, Korea, most of the Asian countries.

He was fourth generation Japanese/American. He was a reasonably contented bachelor, but often remembered his childhood in a cold, dreary Colorado concentration camp. Like many, his grudge was small but intense. Yet, he believed in the United States Constitution, more so than the Americans that shoved his family and himself into the camp at Manzanar.

"Why do I remember the woman?" Clyde Netsuke asked.

Tettsui and Carver nodded.

"Because she seemed in distress. Walking in such a lovely rain, soft and delicate, not too cold, she did not feel this gentle thing. Only some inner turmoil. It was a feeling I got from her when she stood in the doorway. I wanted to reach out and help her. I do not know why I felt that way."

He was unaware that he often modeled his behavior on some mythic code of the West.

Clyde Netsuke was a man thrilled by the Western movie; his favorite star was Gary Cooper, an old-time, lanky Western star. If *High Noon* were playing anytime on TV, he would close the shop and watch the old black-and-white film. Or if one of his other favorites were on in the morning, say three o'clock, he'd set the alarm and watch.

His shop hours were flexible.

"What time did you see this woman?" Tettsui asked.

"Just a few minutes after the rain began."

"Your shop was open?" Tettsui said.

"No, I had closed for the night. But I was sitting in the darkness, watching an old movie. A Western with Audie Murphy. They're not many good Westerns anymore. The Sacketts on TV perhaps."

Carver nodded. Netsuke would get along well with Raphael De Anza. Both lovers of the Wild West. Was Netsuke a fan of Louis L'Amour's novels? He's ask about that sometime, if circumstances permitted.

"Would you show us," Carver said, "where you were, and where the woman was."

Netsuke nodded and crossed the narrow store. He stood behind one of the glass merchandise cases.

"I was here, sitting here." He pointed to a portable thirteen-inch TV set behind the counter. "I was watching Audie Murphy, and the rain began to fall. As it is now. The shop, as I said, was dark. I had not cranked in the awning at the entrance to the shop. This woman came along and stood under the awning, in the shop entranceway. She was not more than fifteen feet from me."

He went to the shop door and stood next to the closed glass door. On the street pedestrians hurried by, umbrellas against the wind and rain.

"She stood there," Netsuke said, pointing outside. "She turned several times and looked at the display in the window. I could see her clearly, considering the light from the street lamps across—"

The door glass shattered and the top of Netsuke's head exploded in a spray of hair and blood and tissue.

SIXTEEN

The muted sound of the gunshot echoed from across the street. Carver and Tettsui threw themselves down as Clyde Netsuke's body fell back like a grain sack. Two more rapid-fire shots smashed the display window. More glass tinkled madly and mingled with the sound of rain rushing into the shop.

Another two shots! Down low into the glass door. Then a car revved its engine, and tires screamed.

Tettsui jumped to his feet, his 9mm Heckler & Koch automatic in his hand. Carver jerked open the shattered door—to give Tettsui a clear shot. Tettsui slid across the sidewalk. Too late. Down the block the car accelerated through the intersection and out of sight.

On both sides of the wet-shiny street stunned bystanders stood under their umbrellas. Several pointed in the direction of the vanished car. Others huddled in shop doors.

"Damn," Tettsui muttered, and shoved the gun back into his waist holster. He trembled and turned to Carver. "Now—we call the police."

Carver nodded and also trembled. From rage, fear, or shock, he could not tell. He told Tettsui to keep the onlookers from stepping into the curio shop.

He walked to his Chrysler, which was parked close by. He almost dropped the keys his hands shook so badly. Finally he managed to open the car. He took a manila envelope from the glove compartment.

Then he opened the trunk. Two locked metal boxes had been welded to the interior. One contained cameras, various occupational identifications, several night scopes, and a state-of-the-art microphone sweep unit. The other had a Colt Python .357 magnum revolver, cleaning equipment, boxes of ammo, four speed-loaders, and a shoulder holster.

Carver removed the heavy handgun, the holster, ammo, and two speed-loaders. He returned to the shop.

By this time the jabbering pedestrians had gathered. Obviously Mike Tettsui had not had time to call the police. Hoping for the license number of the car, he had asked if anybody had seen the license plates. The crowd dissipated.

"So much for public-spirited cooperation," Tettsui said, as he and Carver crunched through the shattered glass.

They stepped over the body. Carver found the phone behind the counter. One of the display cases had a spray of blood patterned on it, like a flattened flower pressed in a book. As Carver tapped out a number, Tettsui covered Netsuke's body with muslin he found in a back storeroom.

"Bea," Carver said, when Murphy answered, "is everything okay?"

"Of course. You sound worried, lad. Anything wrong?"

"What's Royal doing?"

"I assume she's writing poetry. I think she's trying to find a rhyme for rugged-looking black guy—"

"Did she make any calls after I left?"

"No. She hasn't been near the phone."

"All right. Get her out of there. Fast."

"What's happened?" Murphy asked.

"Later," Carver replied. "Just get her out. I don't want to know where."

"Right. I'll call you later."

Carver hung up, then called the police.

He took off his trench coat and suit coat and put on the shoulder holster. As he chambered a speed-loader, he told Tettsui of his suspicions.

"Someone followed me from the office to the motel to here. And apparently figured out what we were doing here. And killed Mr. Netsuke."

"I got news for you, Carver," Tettsui said. "That guy wasn't just after Mr. Netsuke. Those other shots were meant for us—probably for you."

"Yeah," Carver agreed.

In less than ten minutes the shop was filled with homicide detectives and cops. The forensic team had to push the cops out just to get started.

Sergeant Ernie Ludlow shoved Mike Tettsui and Carver Bascombe into the rear storeroom, which was laden with cardboard boxes. A feeble fluorescent lamp flickered. The stacked cartons were marked with stenciled return addresses from Shanghai, Hong Kong, Papeete, Manila, and other cities. The air had the musty odor of mildewed cardboard and disintegrating cordage.

With Ludlow was another detective—Dan Gulden, a beefy young man, with close-cropped hair. Ludlow had on a well-worn tan raincoat, and Gulden wore a sweater under a sport coat.

Ludlow was in a foul mood. As usual.

Gulden seemed expectant, rubbing his thick hands together, not from the cold, but gleefully as though waiting for good news about someone he despised.

As the police combed the streets for witnesses, Ludlow and Gulden got the story from Carver and Tettsui. Gulden wrote in a notebook, but Carver suspected he also had a tape recorder operating in his pocket. As Carver's own recorder functioned.

Carver kept his story short. He left out personal events concerning Claire and Royal Blue. He left them out as protective coloring, as self-defense. But finally he told Ludlow about the vandalism on Royal Blue's apartment.

"Bascombe," Ludlow said, his voice gravelly and menacing, "I don't like it when you cross me. I told you to stay outta it. Now you tell us there was an attack on this poet—this Royal Blue. Jesus, what a name! On her apartment, for chrissake. Just what the hell did you think you were doin'?"

"What I told you," Carver answered. "Finding an alibi for Laura. The apartment raid might've had nothing to do with this. If I had reported it, a cop would've taken down the particulars and told Blue to inform her insurance company—if she had one."

"Yeah, yeah, but you didn't find this Netsuke guy. Your Jap buddy did." Ludlow turned to Tettsui. "Isn't that right?"

"Yes, that is so." Tettsui was calm, composed.

"So, Bascombe, what were you doin' all the time Tettsui was on the job? Not just talkin' to the poets—no, you were blabbin' your fuckin' brains out to that TV broad. And I had just told you to stay out. You're playin' your games again—"

"Ernie—" Carver began.

"Sergeant, remember?" Ludlow said flatly, "or Sergeant Ludlow. Only those will do. Got it?"

"And listen, asshole," Gulden said to Carver, "just answer the sergeant's questions." He turned to Tettsui. "I don't like PI's who are quick on the trigger. You're damned lucky you didn't get a chance to fire that thing."

"I have a license," Tettsui said, "and I am qualified in over a dozen hand weapons, semiautomatic and full automatic."

"Yeah? You sound like one a those Red Dragon terrorists. Well, this ain't the military, buddy. Straighten up and listen right."

Tettsui nodded. Carver handed the tape cassette from his recorder to Ludlow. He also handed him the contents of the manila envelope he had taken from his glove compartment. Ludlow looked at the dry copies of the news clippings on the death of Olive Beem Dale.

"What the fuck?" Ludlow said.

Gulden read over his superior's shoulder.

"I'll be damned!" Gulden said. "Hare—and before that this Dale poet. Someone's trying to kill off lady poetesses."

"Royal suspected that," Carver said.

"You believe this?" Ludlow asked, his tone of voice saying he didn't.

"It throws doubt on Laura as a viable suspect."

"Jesus," Gulden muttered, "listen to that—'viable' yet."

"Shut up, Dan," Ludlow said. "I can criticize this nigger, but not you. You treat him like you would any citizen."

"What it adds up to," Carver said, "is that Laura has to be innocent. She couldn't have hired someone to kill Netsuke. He was her alibi. You'll have to drop the charges."

"Yeah? Think so?" Gulden said. "You don't tell us what our job is. You don't give us orders. What makes you think Netsuke's killing is in any way connected with the Hare killing? Or this whatsername? Dale? It's possible it's a personal grudge against the guy—"

"No," Carver said. "And Sergeant Ludlow doesn't believe it."

"You won't either," Tettsui added, "when you listen to the tape Carver recorded."

"Who asked you?" Gulden said.

"Shut up, Dan," Ludlow said, flipping the cassette in his hand. "Bascombe, you figured I didn't believe Laura was guilty. Last night you walked away without putting up your usual fuss. That wasn't like you."

Carver nodded.

"Laura De Anza's innocence should not be in doubt," Tettsui added. "Netsuke was her alibi. Why would she kill him? Someone desires her to be the accused. That someone is quite possibly the killer—the murderer you must now seek."

"Maybe it's a double bluff?" Gulden suggested. "It's happened before."

"No, Dan," Ludlow said, then turned to Carver. "For the time being I'll accept your statement that Netsuke saw Laura. I'll listen to the tape, get forensic to check it for authenticity. Then I'll recommend that all charges against Laura be dropped."

"Fuck it," Gulden said, "then it's back to square one. Who's killing these female poets? And why?" He glared at Ludlow. "You going to tell De Anza? That maybe his wife is a possible target for some nutso? And that we got to start over?" He looked at Carver and Tettsui. "So, you two, keep going, get outta here, and don't get in our way. Hear me?"

"We hear you, Detective," Tettsui said.

Carver and Tettsui walked out and got into Carver's car. They decided to see Raphael De Anza, who was probably at work. They parked in the lot behind the Hall of Justice.

Lieutenant De Anza was at his desk, filling out reports. Good wet-weather work. He looked up as the two private detectives entered.

"I just heard the report," he said, and grinned. "I called the captain, and the DA is going to recommend dropping the charges. But this doesn't lift the restriction on me. It's still not my investigation."

De Anza's face brimmed with gratitude, his eyes moist. He wiped a hand across his mustache and blinked his eyes.

"You did great, Carver," he said. His voice was hoarse and choked. "Both of you. Laura and I are in your debt."

De Anza shook Mike Tettsui's hand. His dragged-down look was replaced with energy. De Anza stood straighter, and a small smile of triumph flickered at the corners of his mouth. The pressure of the past forty-eight hours was dissipating. He turned to Carver.

"Now, Carver, let's talk business. Your job is finished.

I'll send you a check immediately—but you bill me for the rest. All right?"

"We'll work it out," Carver said.

"Also, amigo, there are things I wish to speak about—privately. No hard feelings, Mike?"

"Not at all, Lieutenant," Tettsui said. "I understand."

Tettsui walked to the assignment board and studied it.

"I heard about the TV broadcast," De Anza said, once Tettsui was out of earshot. "That Overton is a real *hija de perra.*"

Carver nodded, saying nothing.

"My first impulse," De Anza said, "was to tell you you were fired. Then I realized you were probably waiting for such a call. I'm enough of a reasonable man to allow one mistake. And you couldn't foresee that one."

"Thanks, Raf."

"Okay—I know you didn't come here to tell me what Ludlow is or isn't doing. There's something else."

Carver nodded at De Anza's intuition, which came from a lot of years of experience among the street punks, the liars, the cheats, the killers. There was damn little that De Anza missed. Including the prejudices in his own department. He had been passed over once for promotion to captain.

Carver explained what had happened with Royal Blue, but as with Ludlow, didn't mention Claire Overton's part. De Anza could figure that out and had probably done so already.

Since he hadn't had a chance to think about it, Carver did not mention the meeting with Gordon Dale and JoAnne Stanton. He made a mental note to call Dale later, to see if his offer was still negotiable.

"Ludlow has kept me informed," De Anza said. "Unofficially."

"Did you know he was investigating the other poets who were at Hatt's that night?"

"Not at first. But finally he told me he didn't believe Laura was guilty. So, as far as I'm concerned, your job is finished. But I know you, Carver. . . . You're not going to stop there."

Carver shook his head.

"I didn't think so," De Anza said. "Would it do any good to tell you to stay out of it?"

"Ludlow already did that. I don't have all the answers. I'm going to get them."

"My advice, amigo, is let Ludlow take the ball."

"I've got to know," he said, and added silently he had to see about getting Gordon Dale to pay for the effort.

"Yes, I can see that," De Anza said. "You always were an obsessive guy. Don't you think Ludlow is going to do his job?"

"Not if he just goes after the killer of lady poets."

"Why not? Don't you think someone is trying to kill them?"

"I'm not sure. But someone seems to want us to think so."

Carver and Tettsui drove back to the curio shop. They talked in the car. Carver told Tettsui about the meeting with Gordon Dale and JoAnne Stanton.

"You're going to work for him?"

"Maybe."

"One of them might be—"

"Yeah, I know. So, check them both out. Don't let either Dale or Stanton know, but see if they have alibis for the other night."

"Right, consider it done."

"The cops are going to crawl all over. Interrogating Lorna Stokes, Holliday Kraft—maybe even Laura. They're going to check out Harold Yoshima and Jack Bovee—"

"Remember Ludlow's warning," Tettsui said. "It's your funeral."

Carver merely shrugged and pushed down a tiny smile.

Tettsui told Carver to call him if he needed help. He got out and walked to his own car. Carver headed for Russian Hill. He parked on a steep eastern slope, up from the Art Institute.

He opened a slim book of Jack Bovee's poetry. He memorized several lines. He got out and walked carefully downhill on the wet sidewalk, as the rain gurgled and sucked at his footsteps.

Jack Bovee's address was a basement apartment in a shabby building that looked like it might collapse in the next earthquake. Carver rang the bell, and a long-haired young woman opened the door.

"What do you want?" she demanded.

"Jack Bovee," Carver said, and showed her his ID.

"I don't know if he'll see you," she said flatly. "He's busy. He's a great poet and he guards his valuable time."

"You're the guardian?" he asked.

"Maybe I'm his muse," she said, and shut the door in Carver's face.

After a long moment she opened it again and gestured Carver inside.

"I'm Letitia," the woman said. "And I don't want you to take up a lot of Jack's time. Great poetry belongs to the people, even if they don't know it or understand it. So don't waste his time. Got that?"

"Got it."

Letitia was in her mid-twenties, with small eyes set close together. A measles-like epidemic of freckles swam over one cheek, traversed a beaky nose, flooded over the other cheek, and disappeared beneath lanky strands of hair.

Carver wasn't impressed with the apartment. The walls were damp, and there was a constant smell of wood rot. The decor was bricks and board, Goodwill lamps and chairs. One easy chair leaked stuffing, like a misshapen, mutant, fuzzy animal giving birth to dust balls.

A short, gruff black man with grizzled gray hair stepped out from what was apparently used as a combo living room and workroom. Carver identified himself.

"Come on in, Mr. Bascombe," Jack Bovee said, shaking the PI's hand. "Yosh told me you'd be dropping by. Excuse the mess—haven't had much of a chance to get the place cleaned up." He pointed to a pile of books and papers on a chair. "Just move that stuff onto that table and get comfortable."

Carver heaved the arm load of books and papers onto a worktable, which was already overloaded with papers, books, magazines, drinking glasses, and the remains of a pizza on a cracked plate. The tomato paste looked caked and was probably several days old.

The young woman sat in a chair in a corner.

"You've met Letitia, of course," Bovee said. "She's a sort of one-poet groupie. I'm just mighty glad she's attracted to me—as I am to her. However, you're interested in answers, as Yosh informed me. I'm looking forward to our chat. Yes, I certainly am."

Despite the gray hair, Carver guessed Bovee was only in his forties. Bovee seemed self-satisfied. Or was it arrogance? A pair of spectacles rested on the top of his head, and another pair was folded into the V-top of the thick maroon sweater he wore. Carver wondered why the two pair of glasses.

Carver looked around the apartment: two rooms and a kitchen. Old and dilapidated. A faint smell of mildew drifted in the air and tickled Carver's nose. One of the rain-streaked windows leaked a puddle onto the floor. He didn't see many books on shelves and figured the poet kept them, perhaps, in the bedroom. Removed from the danger of getting wet.

No TV set; Bovee apparently didn't watch television. Which was fine with Carver. Less chance of Bovee having seen Claire Overton's program or the news of the killing of Clyde Netsuke. He didn't see a radio either. Odd.

Letitia smiled at Carver, a weak, disinterested smile, and then at Jack Bovee, a full-blown I-worship-at-the-feet-of-a-god smile.

"Now, tell us what's going on," Bovee said, settling himself into the overstuffed mutant chair. "Tell me, Carver, why you're looking into this murder. And what can I do to help?"

Carver told him a little; he asked Bovee's opinion of Laura De Anza and Geraldine Hare. The poet's views on Laura's personality were about the same as Stokes's, Yoshima's, and Kraft's. His version of the fight between Laura and Hare was the same. Everything fit.

"I wasn't there," Letitia finally said.

Carver didn't ask if Bovee thought Laura killed Hare; the black poet's opinion hardly counted at this stage.

There was something about Bovee that was artificial. It was as though he were acting a role, the jolly, hail-fellow-well-met, friendly, yet urbane. Carver needed to trip Jack Bovee.

"Did you know Holliday Kraft was a prostitute?"

Bovee paused in the act of wiping one pair of his glasses. He was caught off base. Letitia giggled.

"Holly?" he said, widening his eyes. "Really? What makes you think so? No, forget I asked, bro'. I'm sure you have your reasons to think so." He thought for long moments before speaking again. "What Holly does to make a living takes none of the edge off her poetry. She's an excellent poet. She deserves her place in our new anthology. Please—go on."

"Did you see Laura later that night?"

"The night Gerry was stabbed? No, no, I didn't see her after she left Hatt's. I went for a walk with Yosh—down to Aquatic Park. I've always liked the dark waters of the bay. It's in my poetry, if you've ever read any of it."

Carver lied, said he hadn't. Some instinct told him to give Bovee nothing, no advantage.

"I guess you might say we're a strange bunch," Bovee volunteered. "Even strange for a passel of poets. I've always thought there should be some official word for a gathering of poets. Like a gathering of lions is called a pride of lions. Or a covey of pigeons, or a herd of cattle. I really should put my mind to it. Get a word that would go into Webster's dictionary."

"Did you know Olive Dale?"

"Blunt aren't you? Well, I suppose that's some kind of good investigating technique. For instance I've noticed you don't call anyone by their name. Do you suppose it's some kind of phobia, so you don't get too close to a person? That it might be a means of keeping your distance? From what, I don't know, since I really don't know you at all. Ever ask yourself these questions, Carver?" He snuggled down in the easy chair, adjusting his glasses on the end of his nose. "You'll notice I've been calling you by your first name. I think that sort of establishes a friendlier relationship between us."

Carver nodded and studied the older man.

"Of course," Bovee continued, "it's only because poets

see things different. We're always concerned with ourselves and our environment. It's our eternal struggle to exist in a world that gives damn-all about poetry. It's not exactly something you'll see on TV. None of that play-off stuff in the world of poets. And it's probably too personal. TV doesn't do well with intense personal stuff. Not even on PBS stations."

He gestured around the small, unkempt apartment.

"See, I'm talking about TV, and I don't own a set. Well, Carver, I used to, and I realized I was wasting a lot of time watching it. And that took away from my work with words." He cocked his head and gestured a finger in the air, as if he were some old-time orator. "Poetry, my friend, is a way of telling a story in the least possible words. A novelist can go on for hundreds and hundreds of pages, but a poet takes the same property and condenses it, distills it, mutates it into the many layers of human experience. 'Adam had em.' The story of fleas. See what I'm saying?"

Carver shrugged a quarter of an inch and nodded slightly.

"Oh, good," Bovee said, "the strong silent type. You say you haven't read my poetry. Have you read the work of the others in the group?"

Carver shrugged noncommittally.

"Oh, Jack's poetry is wonderful," Letitia said, the words almost gushing.

> *"Coal skin, seen as the color of evil*
> *but it is a cry of hue, a game of dye*
> *of rules made by others in another life—"*

"It's an interesting game you and I are playing, isn't it?" Bovee asked. "Sort of a standoff. All this talk gets me curious. You come here, introduce yourself, and ask questions about Hare and Laura De Anza, and tell me Kraft is a hooker—"

"Call girl," Carver said.

"All right, call girl, and judging from where she lives, a very high-priced one, too. Which lets me out of her action, as you can see." Bovee gestured at the shabby furnishings in the apartment. "And I don't mind admitting I'd like one night with her. Wouldn't you?" Bovee narrowed his eyes at Carver, a slight leer twisting his face. "Or are you one of those brothers that doesn't hanker for a white woman?"

Carver said nothing.

"I don't think I'd like that, Jack," Letitia said. "Aren't I enough for you? I'm white. And I doubt if Holliday would do as much, with as much love as I give you, Jack. Don't you think she'd only be a momentary release for you? She wouldn't share a deeply intimate affair—as you and I have?"

"Don't worry about it, lover," Bovee said. He turned to Carver. "A lot of the brothers don't like it when blacks get together with whites. Sexually, you understand. A black poet said, Clarence Major said, something like—'The black poet must chop away at the white criterion and destroy its hold on his black mind because seeing the world through white eyes from inside a black soul causes death. . . .' What do you think?"

Carver shrugged.

"Man, you are a tough one to talk to." Bovee's exasperation was a bit exaggerated. "So talk to me. You have questions, I got questions. Quid pro quo? We both get answers. Okay?"

"All right."

"Good, Carver, good. Now what about the official police? Shouldn't they be conducting this investigation?"

"Yes."

"Yes," Bovee mimicked, dragging out the word. "I've already been visited by a brother—one ugly detective named Sergeant Ludlow. I can see where the cops might blunder around. Aren't those your thoughts also?"

"No."

"And you believe Laura innocent?"

Again Carver shrugged.

"Well, I'm afraid I can be of little help," Bovee said. "I certainly never saw her after she left Hatt's that night."

"Someone else might have a motive for killing Geraldine Hare."

"Hmmm, yes, it's possible—although for the life of me I

109

can't imagine who it would be. Or the motive. Have any of the other poets said anything that might open up that avenue of investigation?''

"Like who?''

"Oh—maybe Lorna Stokes? I'd say there's more to Lorna than meets the eye. I could tell you things about Lorna—yes, I could, Carver, but . . .''

Carver had heard enough digressions. It was difficult to get Bovee to stay on a subject and answer questions. He had not answered Carver's question about Olive Beem Dale.

"I'll ask this again—did you know Olive Dale? Or her husband?''

"Who? Oh, yes, Olive Dale.'' Bovee stroked his face, took off his glasses, and chewed on the stems. "I guess I do ramble. Yes, Olive Beem Dale. I know of her, of course, but I've never met the woman or her husband. I do recall that Yosh mentioned he might ask her to join our group. Yes, of course, because—because Geraldine Hare had threatened to quit.''

"But Jack,'' Letitia said, "Olive Dale is dead. I remember her, and I remember reading something in the paper . . . a few weeks ago—''

"God—you're right, Letitia!'' Bovee said. "I don't believe this! Dale is dead. Hare is dead.'' He turned to Carver with renewed interest. "Just what is this, Carver? Is there some kind of connection between the two deaths?''

"It's a possibility.''

"That can't be,'' Bovee said. "No, I remember now—the paper said it was an accident. So why should it be connected . . . yet it seems strange that two poets should die within a few weeks of each other?''

"It's horrible,'' Letitia said, and shuddered.

"God, think, think of it,'' Bovee said, and shook his head. "No male poets have been murdered, so it appears some mad creature is stalking and killing female poets.'' He looked up, surprised. "God! Are the others—are they all at risk, in extreme danger?''

Carver shrugged. Watching. Eyes narrowed.

"Then perhaps,'' Bovee mused, "one of us is a suspect. I might be some kind of latter-day Jack the Ripper.''

110

"That's a possibility," Carver admitted.

"That's not something to joke about," Bovee said sullenly—then he brightened. "I think I have you figured out now, Carver, the way you think. I respect you for it, bro'. You won't come out and make a statement until you're sure of your facts. But you'll sucker us in, let us babblers in the world of words talk and talk, on and on. . . . Perhaps one of us will say something out of kilter, and thus become suspects ourselves. I admire that, Carver, I truly do."

Carver figured there was not much to say. But something nagged at his consciousness. For another minute he made small talk, then thanked Jack Bovee and Letitia and made his way out.

Something bothered him. Something Bovee had said? What? Or was it Bovee's performance—for performance it was. Not rehearsed, but not real either, as though Bovee were another person.

He walked up the slippery slope to his car. As he drove down into North Beach toward the Par-Cheesey Pizza shop where Lorna Stokes worked, his mental gears finally meshed. It hit him.

He quickly pulled into the curb on Columbus Avenue then thumbed the rewind of his recorder. He held the machine to his ear and listened. Yes, there it was. He rewound it again.

. . . Gerry was stabbed? No, no, I didn't see her after she left Hatt's. I went for a walk with Yosh—down to Aquatic Park. I've always liked the dark waters of the bay. . . .

Carver grinned to himself. Finally! Finally someone had slipped. Jack Bovee had lied.

Jack Bovee had lied about his whereabouts with Harold Yoshima. Carver remembered clearly: Yoshima had said he and Bovee had taken a walk along Broadway, to Enrico's. Bovee had said they strolled down to Fisherman's Wharf.

One of them was lying—or both of them. Which one lied, and why?

Carver gunned the engine; the wheels slipped in the wet gutter then pulled into traffic. He turned at the next corner and headed back to Jack Bovee's apartment.

He'd park across the street and go into surveillance. He'd

watch and see what Jack Bovee did and where he went. In the pouring rain he doubted if he'd be noticed.

The dreary day looked like it might be a test of patience.

SEVENTEEN

As Carver turned the corner, he glanced up the slope—and saw Jack Bovee and Letitia leave the apartment. They shared an umbrella and dressed in dark gray raincoats, but they were recognizable.

They hadn't seen him. Not in the rain. And neither Bovee nor Letitia had previously seen the Chrysler. Carver drove past; he wouldn't have to endure a tedious, cold-and-wet stakeout. He made a U-turn at the top of the street and drove downhill again.

They were out of sight, but at the intersection he spotted them to his right, about a quarter-way up the block. Bovee and Letitia turned into an alley.

He parked at a fire hydrant, the only available space. Staying close to the building at the alley entrance, he watched them stand in front of a two-car garage. Bovee looked furtively about, then fingered a remote garage-door opener. The wide door lifted.

What the hell? Carver forced his questions down. Watch and learn.

A black Bentley slid out of the garage. As the door closed,

Carver moved back and stepped into a doorway. The Bentley turned left and headed up the hill.

Carver scrambled into his car. In less than fifteen seconds he was about ten car-lengths behind. Even with the Chrysler's wipers smearing the windshield, the English-built car was easy to follow. Jack Bovee was not a speeder.

Bovee turned west on Union Street, rolled up and over the crest of the hill, and crossed Van Ness Avenue. Carver followed. Beyond Gough Street the Bentley turned and continued majestically uphill, to Pacific Heights. The Bentley turned into a long driveway that led to a small mansion with a separate two-car garage.

Carver parked on the opposite side of the street. Through the rain, he studied the mansion that dominated the corner.

Huddled under the umbrella, Jack Bovee and Letitia hurried up a brick walkway to the mansion and let themselves in.

Carver's brow furrowed. They had keys? Who were they going to visit? Why was the expensive car at their disposal? And why was the Bentley parked in a garage near Bovee's basement apartment?

He recorded his questions and formed some possible answers.

The mansion was small as mansions go, with maybe ten or twelve rooms, Carver guessed. Four Corinthian-style pillars fronted the entrance, and tall, narrow windows spilled amber light onto a border of bright perennial flowers. Lawns swept down to a wall, which was about chest-high from the sidewalk.

Carver left his car, jammed the knitted cap to his ears, and crossed the street. At the door he pressed the bell inset into baroque decoration. Footsteps echoed across the inner floor.

Jack Bovee opened the door, his mouth formed an O, and his eyes widened. He carried a cardboard carton filled with papers and files.

"Jack, just a few more questions," Carver said. "If you don't mind?"

"How . . . ? You . . . you followed us?"

Carver nodded and stepped inside. The furnishings were

113

luxurious—what there was of them. The house was curiously empty. A chandelier had once hung in the hallway, but now there was just the empty fixture in the ceiling. Between a bad eighteenth-century Dutch painting, and an obscure nineteenth-century New York impressionist painting (both originals, Carver assumed) were several pale rectangles. Paintings had once hung there.

Winds blew raindrops into the hall and pushed at Carver's trench coat.

More switches clicked in his mind. The too-crummy apartment (like a stage design)—the furtiveness at the garage—the hidden Bentley—all the pieces suggested a possibility. . . .

"This is your place, isn't it?" Carver asked.

"Uh, no, no, this belongs to a friend," Bovee said.

Letitia strolled in, eating a sandwich in one hand, the other carrying a plastic garbage bag.

"Hey, Jack, the draft back here is terrible. Close the door—"

She stopped dead when she saw Carver, and the bag slipped from her fingers onto the marble floor. It spilled paper trash. Gusts of wind from the open doorway scattered most of it down the hallway.

"Hello, Letitia," Carver said and turned again to Bovee. "You lied to me."

"What? What do you mean?" Bovee said, putting down the cardboard carton.

"Throw him out, Jack!" Letitia said, spraying bits of chewed bread, lettuce, and pinkish meat from her lips. "He's trespassing! You didn't invite him in. He just walked in. It's your right."

"No, Letitia," Carver said. "You can't throw me out. Not if you and Jack are just guests. The owner of the house can ask me to leave—and I'll leave."

While Bovee twisted his mouth wordlessly and removed his glasses, Carver strolled casually into the spacious front room. He turned and faced Bovee and Letitia. She was rigid, and her mouth was colored with a smear of mustard. The poet rubbed a hand nervously over his face.

114

"Yeah, you lied," Carver said. "You said you and Yo-shima had walked to—"

"You fucker!" Letitia yelled. "You shit-eating bastard!"

She flung the half-eaten sandwich at Carver. And snarling, she moved forward in a crouch. Her hands were knotted into mishappen fists.

Carver narrowed his eyes.

She drop-kicked a leg at his crotch. He swung to one side, grabbed the fast-moving foot with one hand—and twisted her off balance. She fell to the carpeted floor.

"Hey!" Bovee shouted.

Letitia scrambled around, growling, and almost made it to her feet. Carver backhanded her across the face. Letitia went down. He wiped mustard from the back of his hand and turned to Bovee, who had gone into an attack stance.

"Try it," Carver said hoarsely, "but she's not hurt."

"You sonuvabitch," Bovee muttered.

He sounded frustrated. He went to Letitia and helped her to her feet. He stroked her cheek where Carver had struck her. She glared at Carver, who continued talking.

"Let's get back to that night, Bovee. You told me you and Harold Yoshima walked to Fisherman's Wharf after the fight at Hatt's."

"That's right," Bovee said roughly.

"Yoshima said the two of you had taken a walk into North Beach and stopped off at Enrico's. Who's lying? Fisherman's Wharf, or Enrico's? That's about a ten- or twelve-block difference. It doesn't matter which of you lied, but it means neither of you has an alibi for that night."

"Oh, man, is that all," Bovee said. "We did go to Fisherman's Wharf—then turned around and strolled back up Columbus Avenue, then we had coffee at Enrico's. Hey, bro', it's only about ten minutes from the Wharf to Broadway."

"Yeah—bro'," Carver said.

He made mental tracks of the scene: the ten-minute walk back would pass them close to the scene where Geraldine was murdered. And the time fit.

"You didn't see anyone from the group?"

115

"No. Neither of us did. Yosh and I were together all that time."

All too pat. Carver didn't like it; his hunter's instincts didn't like it. Bovee was lying. He couldn't prove it, but he felt it.

And if Bovee lied . . . then . . .

"If that's all," Bovee said, "then get the hell out."

"This is your house," Carver said.

"So what, bro'?"

"Don't 'brother' me. You're leading a double life."

"Like I said, so what?"

"You're not the working-class poet you profess."

Bovee glared, but the anger died in his eyes. He slumped and then sat in a brocade antique chair. Letitia stood by his side and stroked his grizzled hair.

"I guess it had to come out," he said.

"Tell me about it," Carver prompted gently.

"What's to say?" The poet sounded deflated, defeated. "You're going to tell the world, I suppose."

Carver shrugged.

"You're a cold sucker, aren't you?" Bovee said. "I guess it doesn't make much difference." He gestured at the room of antique furniture, at the luxurious drapes, the gilt coffee tables. "It belonged to my aunt, on my mother's side. She married this wealthy white guy, very successful in the electronics business—but he died about five years ago. My aunt died about a year ago, and I inherited it. A regular white elephant."

"A lot of upkeep," Carver guessed.

"Damn right! I've had to sell things off from time to time. I've tried to sell the place, but it's old, doesn't have a lot of modern conveniences." He paused . . . "And it has a bad foundation. The seller has to pay the costs of bringing the foundation up to code. Do you have any idea what it would cost for this house?"

"Couldn't refinance?"

"With what as collateral? I've never had a steady job. Just temporary work in the blue-collar world. I've always enjoyed that. But as a black man, believe me, the wealthy neighbors around here would just enjoy their asses off to see me slide under. Then they could pick up this real estate for a song. They didn't like my aunt either—a black woman nobbing with the rich white folks. You know what I mean?''

"Yeah," Carver said, remembering the efforts of some of his neighbors to buy him out.

"Believe him, Carver," Letitia said after a time. "Owning this place is Jack's pain in the ass. We're trying to get a civic group to buy it, turn it into some kind of museum. But so far, no luck.''

"They're stalling," Bovee added, "waiting for me to drop the price or to give it up to taxes.''

Carver wondered if Yoshima would tell much the same story, about the walk to Fisherman's Wharf and back into North Beach. He'd have to ask him again. He made a mental note—immediately after talking to Lorna Stokes again, he'd see Harold Yoshima. If the cops hadn't got to him first.

"Well?" Letitia said. "Are you going to be a real asshole and tell the whole world about Jack's misfortune? Or are you going to give him a break?''

Carver said nothing and kept his expression neutral. Let her think what she wanted. And even if he had made a decision, he certainly wouldn't tell Letitia or Jack. Despite the sad song, Jack Bovee was somehow not right. Carver's instinct was running on autopilot.

He made up his mind. Carver reached for the phone. He'd call Rose, see if she had returned from her research in the library.

"Carver, I'm telling you the truth," Bovee said, his tone pleading, and he plucked at Carver's sleeve. "Please. I can only throw myself on your mercy—''

There was a sudden movement.

Bovee struck him!

Carver staggered, dropped the phone, and grabbed at his head. His skull felt thunderous. Blood poured between his fingers. He got a glimpse of Bovee. Arm raised.

Something heavy. In his hand. Paperweight!

Carver stumbled to one side, blocking any attack with one hand, trying to draw the Python with the other.

He saw him coming again. The marble paperweight in one upraised hand. Screaming!

Carver rolled over, seeing red. Blood. Oozing into his eyes. He wiped the thick fluid away—and fired one round at Bovee.

The man yelled and dropped the paperweight.

Letitia grabbed Bovee around the middle, yelling at him, and held him back. She kicked and shouted obscenities and struggled. Holding on. Bovee yelled he wanted to kill the black bastard!

Somehow it seemed incongruous. His screeching racial curses, and his lover holding on. Carver struggled to get up, his revolver wavering in their direction.

He managed to get to his knees, and backed off, feeling somehow like a two-year-old child learning to crawl. The marble felt slick under his hands. The gunpowder smell scratched into the back of his throat.

Bovee managed to scramble from Letitia's grasp. He still had the paperweight. He pushed Letitia aside.

"Don't," Carver said hoarsely.

Bovee threw the weight and Carver fired.

The poet spun out of sight, and Carver felt a shock strike him in the face. Inky blackness rose up like a powerful sewer and swallowed him. He yelled to himself, but the sound was all in his head.

Carver slumped to the floor, his head bleeding on the clean marble.

The ugliness reared up, smothered him. A dim light reached out, casting luminous pallid rays through a fog. All in his mind.

Carver groaned. He twisted and felt the cold marble floor on either side of him. Wet. Sticky.

Something was making some kind of noise. Little shrieking sounds.

He rolled onto one side and almost threw up from the pain. Probably a concussion for sure. Nausea did that. The ringing wouldn't stop.

He opened one eye. The other felt caked shut with blood.

The ringing went on.

The pager.

He reached to his belt and thumbed it off. He managed that action one-handed. The Python was still in his right hand. Carver shoved it into his holster.

Grunting, he pushed himself across the floor, almost gliding in his own blood. Another suit ruined. And this time he'd have to send the trench coat to the cleaners.

He reached for the phone on the floor and tapped out the paging service. Rose was trying to reach him. The time dragged and seemed to drift farther from reality, but he called her.

"You sound terrible, Boss," Rose said.

"Mmuunh—yuuh," Carver said.

He forced himself to stop mumbling, told her the address, and told her to come and get him. Bring first aid.

"Be right there," she said. "I've got hot information. You'll love it."

He hung up and managed to prop himself up against the wall. Apparently none of the neighbors had heard the shooting. Otherwise he'd be ass-deep in cops.

He looked at the floor. A couple of blood spots. He didn't remember crawling that far. No. He hadn't. He scanned the floor—trash littered it from the bag Letitia had dropped. He eyeballed a series of red spatters going to the front door.

Damn! He'd managed to hit either Bovee or Letitia. Probably Bovee.

Something worked into his mind, a plump, malformed message, like a brutalized bubble from a polluted pond. What was it? Something he remembered? Why couldn't he remember what was nagging at him?

What could anyone expect, with a bashed-in head? That was one advantage of having kinky hair—it was good cushioning material. That—and his knitted watch cap. Otherwise he'd be in a coma—or dead. Probably.

He needed to clear his head. He pushed himself erect and staggered past the dining room into the kitchen. At the sink he splashed water on his face. He dried himself with a dish towel.

He felt better and relaxed into a ladder-back kitchen chair.

Carver let his mind drift over the past several days. He conjured up various scenes, and he particularly enjoyed the ones with Royal Blue. Was that it? Something about Royal? No. Stokes? No. Kraft? No. Yoshima? Gordon Dale? No. And not Stanton either . . .

Wait. Back up a bit. Yoshima.

He pushed his memory back to the talk with Yoshima. There was indeed something there. Assume Yoshima lied, he thought—his head ached. It escaped him.

"Hey, boss!" Rose's voice shouted. "You up and around?"

Carver called out, and she entered the kitchen. She took one look at Carver and whistled. Rose opened the metal first-aid kit. With a glass of water she made Carver swallow two pills.

"Percodan," she said. "I thought that other beating you took was bad. Are you sure you're alive?"

"Barely."

"Who did this? Bovee?"

Carver told her briefly, as she took out bandages and antiseptic from a large handbag. He brought her up to date on events—Dale and Stanton, and Netsuke.

"Let's leave it to the cops, boss," she said as she tended his wounds. "This is getting bad."

"No—what did you find out?"

"I know about Bovee and this house," Rose said, and taped a final bandage to his head. "He's leading a double life. The apartment is a front, a sort of safe house. If I'd dug deeper into the city records, I'd probably find out he owns the whole building."

"I figured that," Carver said. "There was pizza on the table in that crummy apartment that had to be a week old. Hardly anyone would leave that around—unless it was by design. A set. A stage set."

"And Bovee shot Laura's alibi? Netsuke?"

"No—I doubt it. I saw Bovee shortly after the shooting. He didn't have the right feel—he wasn't that cold-blooded.

He's more emotional. After killing Netsuke, the killer shot at me."

"Come on! Why?"

"Somebody thinks I know more than I know."

"Maybe, or else you're just getting in the way."

Carver nodded. God, his head hurt!

"I've got to find Bovee's trail," he said. "Maybe he left something in this house—"

"I doubt that," Rose said, and opened one of several thick letter-sized manila envelopes. "I'll start with this stuff—Jack Bovee's property—"

"Yeah, I know. It's heavily mortgaged. A white elephant—inherited from his aunt, on his mother's side. So much for the working-class poet."

"Oh, he's got a double life, no doubt about that—but, Boss, everything else is screwed up. He didn't inherit that house."

He raised an eyebrow.

"He bought it ten years ago. And he just sold it, a week ago. As is. It isn't his anymore."

Carver was too exhausted to react.

"God, Bovee can really lie," he said.

"First," Rose said, "according to incorporation records, Bovee, DBA JayVeeBee Enterprises, owned a computer company that was going broke. The company was a source of programmed software but couldn't keep up with all the technological advances. More aggressive firms brought out better software. Mostly JayVeeBee Enterprises put all their bets on basic programs for CP/M—"

"Which got clobbered when IBM made MS/DOS the prevalent program."

"Yes, you got that figured out. How come you know so much about computers and we don't even have one in the office? Have you been holding out on me?"

"Rose, I promise, we'll get you a computer. But first let's search this place. It's obvious that Bovee was moving out."

As they went from room to room, Rose finished her report.

"Bovee started selling things from this mansion and from

other sources to keep his company alive. Finally he sold the mansion and everything in it.''

"Which probably made his neighbors happy."

"I don't know anything about that," Rose said as they searched the upstairs bedrooms. "It's not part of public records."

"Bigotry never is," Carver said. "Did you get anything from Herb Randall—about Harold Yoshima?"

"Not yet. But Herb promised to call as soon as he got anything about him. Herb says he knows the name but can't place it. I didn't tell him Yoshima was a poet, figuring the less information he had, the fewer preconceptions. It'd keep his mind open."

"All right," Carver said.

The upstairs was empty. Carver looked in trash baskets. They were clean. Nothing upstairs yielded anything. They came downstairs.

"I have to know one thing, Carver," Rose said. "If someone is killing off the female poets—then where does the killing of Netsuke fit in? Why let Laura off the hook? Why destroy her alibi? It would only make the cops suspicious. As it has. Why not let the cops continue to think she killed Hare?"

"Because the killer wants the cops to follow another lead."

"But killing Mr. Netsuke in broad daylight was a terrible risk. Why do they want us to go down that trail? Bovee—and who was the dame—?"

"Letitia—no known last name. Yet."

He closed his eyes, denying the pain that tumbled through his head. He remembered—when he first entered the house, winds had scattered paper which Letitia had dropped.

"Bovee knows he's on the spot," Rose said, continuing her scenario. "Now he's on the run. He knew you were coming to see him—so he calls someone—and that person follows you from our office to the motel. Then the killer tries to kill you after shooting Mr. Netsuke—to prevent you from talking to Bovee?"

"Yeah," Carver said, and searched the hallway for anything Letitia and Bovee might have missed.

"That makes Bovee the killer's accomplice," Rose said. "Which also means their timetable, whatever it is, is winding down. We've got to catch up."

The hallway was still littered with much of the trash. Carver and Rose Weinbaum went down on their knees and looked through all of it. They scanned every scrap. He found several pieces with names and telephone numbers.

"Who are they?" Rose asked. "Poets?"

"James Dudley—Frank Needlemeier—Gerald McKinnon. I've never heard of any of them if they are."

Carver telephoned the first man, Dudley, who identified himself as a supplier of computer accessories. Dudley had done business with JayVeeBee Enterprises, but had never met any of the executives. Business was done from catalog sales. Dudley said his company had not had an order from JayVeeBee in over four months.

The second man, Frank Needlemeier, was cautious.

"Who did you say you were?" Needlemeier asked.

Carver identified himself, but Needlemeier wasn't buying it.

"How did you get this number?" he asked.

"From Jack Bovee's house."

"I'm afraid I don't understand—"

"I'd like to know about JayVeeBee Enterprises."

"I've never done business with them."

Something about Needlemeier's voice—his denial was far too cautious.

"I can't blame you for being suspicious, Mr. Needlemeier," Carver said, pleasant and unthreatening, "so I'm going to give you a name for reference. Do you know Mr. Herb Randall of Tan-ta-Mount Logic?"

Warily, Needlemeier said he was familiar with the name.

"Good. Call Randall and ask him about Carver Bascombe. Then call me back. Randall has my number."

"I'll think about it," Needlemeier said and hung up.

"What was that all about?" Rose asked.

Carver waved away an answer. He wasn't sure.

The third person he called—McKinnon—was a public-relations man. JayVeeBee had inquired about some publicity—about four months ago. McKinnon had never met any of the officers of the corporation and certainly no one named Bovee. Nothing there, Carver decided.

Carver wrote the name Needlemeier in his notebook. He and Rose left the big house and got into Carver's car.

"Where to now, Boss?" Rose asked.

"To see Lorna Stokes."

"Good. She's got a lot of questions to answer." Meaningfully Rose tapped the large manila envelope she carried. "So drive."

"We have to move fast," Carver said, driving carefully in the rain. "The cops are going to swarm over Yoshima, Holliday Kraft, and Stokes. And maybe even Laura again. If they've bought the idea that the lady poets are in danger."

"Don't you think it's true?" Rose asked.

"Options are open."

"Good, Boss. Don't take anything for granted." She rummaged in the manila envelope. "Now about Lorna Stokes—She's the franchised owner of the Par-Cheesey shop in North Beach."

Carver turned and stared at Rose. Then forced his attention back to his driving. His head throbbed unmercifully.

"She owns that shop?" he asked.

"That's what the City Hall records say. And makes a damn good living at it."

"Then why does she drive pizzas around?"

"Well, she's got the shop mortgaged to the hilt. I called in a marker from a banker friend of mine. She's in the red, financially."

"Yeah, it makes sense. She's a crack user. She probably has the shop in hock to pay for the cocaine. But it doesn't explain why she still delivers pizzas." He thought for a moment. "But I think I know. We'll get the answers in just a few seconds."

Carver pulled to the curb a half block from the Par-Cheesey shop.

EIGHTEEN

The Par-Cheesey shop was warm and steamy. Condensation glazed the windows. Cooked tomato smells mingled with the yeasty odor of rising dough. Stronger aromas of spices, sausage, and pepperoni tantalized the air.

"I'm sorry sir," the lady cashier said to Carver, "but we can't tell you our drivers' routes."

The cashier was a woman in her early fifties and prone to putting on weight.

"I just can't do that," she said. "I'm sorry."

"You'll be sorrier," Rose said. "Do you have any idea what the sentence is for obstructing justice?"

"Now see here," the cashier said, "I don't have to listen to that. You and this gentleman are not the police—"

"You've seen our licenses," Rose said.

"Yes, but that can't force me to answer you. I know my constitutional rights. I don't have to tell you where Miss Stokes is."

"Oh? You're right on that score," Rose said. "So let's talk about her alibi. The cops wanted to know where she was the night Geraldine Hare was killed. You told Sergeant Ludlow she was here when the rain started. You lied to police."

Beads of sweat dotted the woman's upper lip and her forehead—whether from worry or the warmth of the shop was difficult to judge.

A young man came out from the kitchen. He identified himself as the manager. Carver remembered Lorna Stokes telling him the manager was younger. He told him he wanted Stokes's route listing.

"I see, I see," the manager repeated, quite worried. "I see."

"The employees here gave Miss Stokes an alibi. The cops don't like lies."

"Well, I'm the manager . . . but we . . . I . . ."

"You don't own the place," Carver said, and weaved slightly from pain and nausea. "We know."

"Anyway, it wasn't a lot of police. Only one detective, a big black guy. Sergeant Ludlow, I believe."

"How could you forget?" Rose said.

The door opened, and Lorna Stokes came in. She stopped and blinked at the cashier, the young manager, then at Carver Bascombe. She started to leave, then apparently thought better of it. She walked to the cash register and put down a number of bills, along with receipts.

"Deposit those, Dwight," she said to the manager.

"Yes, Miss Stokes," he said, and avoided looking at Rose and Carver.

Stokes wore the clothes she had worn before: shapeless plastic rain hat, dark skirt, heavy sweater, and a quilted blue jacket.

"Nice to see you again, Carver. What brings you out on a day like this? A craving for pizza?"

"No," Carver said.

"Ooh, we're back to being monosyllabic, are we? I figured it was only a matter of time before you'd be back. I'd already had enough of that other cop, that black guy with the rough manner. He sure never read any poetry."

"We have to talk," Carver said, and introduced Rose.

"I don't think we have time, Bascombe. I got pizzas to deliver."

"Get one of your other drivers to do it."

"My other—? Oh." She paused, then looked at the manager, who nodded ashamedly to her. "I see. You think you know something?"

"I know about Jack Bovee."

Lorna Stokes looked puzzled, knitting her brows together. She shook her head, then took a list of orders from a shelf. She called into the kitchen and was handed a stack of pizzas in a warming carton.

"You want to talk, we can talk in the car. I got to deliver these pizzas, whether you like it or not. Remember what I said, about rainy days, especially nights—the people don't want to go out, they want piping-hot pizzas brought right to their doors. And the orders don't wait for no man. Or woman."

She laughed and, carrying the heavy carton, went out the door. Carver and Rose followed and got into the old compact car. Rose sat in the rear seat, next to the warming carton.

Stokes shoved the car into gear and shot off down the wet street. She maneuvered the car expertly, quickly, as she had before. Carver held on.

"So what's up?" Stokes asked.

"You lied," Carver said.

"That's my concern."

"You don't seem worried."

She shrugged and said nothing. She pulled to the curb and grabbed a pizza from the carton.

"Be right back," she said, "and then maybe we can iron this out."

"I'm going with you," Carver said.

"Nah, you're not. You think I'm going to run out? Forget it. I know what I'm doing. I have nothing to worry about. I'll be back right quick."

With that Lorna Stokes went into an apartment building and was back in less than five minutes. She grinned at Carver and Rose then consulted her delivery list. Again, she gunned the engine and roared up a steep hill, the car's tires spinning on the rainy asphalt.

"Lorna," Carver began, "we know you own the shop."

"Yes, really? I do? How do you figure that?"

"It's a matter of public record," Rose Weinbaum explained. "It's part of the papers you had to file at City Hall."

"Oh, I see," Stokes said, nodding. "Well, I won't deny it. But it's something I didn't want to get around. I have my reputation as a working-woman's poet. I don't want it ruined, and you can surely understand that."

"You deliver pizzas to keep up that reputation."

"Yes, I do."

"Jack Bovee had a similar situation. I don't like coincidences."

"Again with Bovee. You've got one hell of a fixation on Jack. Look, he's just a good poet. Poor as a sewer rat, but dedicated to the art of poetry."

She seemed sincere in her estimation of Bovee. Carver was puzzled. Was there something he had missed? He didn't think so. Yet Lorna Stokes was sure of herself. He needed to rattle her cage.

"You use crack," Carver said.

Caught off guard, Lorna darted her eyes at him. They grew large, then dimmed. She chuckled.

"So what? It's just recreational. I can take care of it."

"Sure," Carver said. Disbelieving. "But you're in trouble because of it. That's why you deliver pizzas. One of these addresses is a base house, where you get the crack."

"That's a joke," she said, a beading of perspiration forming on her forehead. "I don't think you can prove that."

"I don't have to," Carver said. "And I don't want to."

"What? Why?"

"I'm only interested in the murder of Geraldine Hare. And of Olive Dale. Jack Bovee is mixed up in it, and he's dangerous."

"Oh, Christ, don't tell me you believe that stuff about someone trying to kill off female poets that belonged to the group? And you think I'm in some kind of danger? It's all a lot of hooey. Forget that."

"Jack Bovee—" Carver began.

"Has nothing to do with anything," Stokes said emphatically. "I'm telling you—Olive Dale's death was an accident. Just that, an accidental fall. As for Geraldine Hare, well, I don't know who killed her. If it wasn't Laura, then I'd think it was Hare's lesbian lover."

"Do you know the name?"

"Who? Gerry's lover? I met her once. A blond dyke—but I don't recall her name. But you're going up the wrong street."

She pulled into the curb and retrieved another pizza from the backseat. She told them she'd be back.

"We got a lot to talk about—and it isn't about me using an occasional taste of the white lady. That has nothing to do with any of this." She laughed, a kind of deep chuckle. "No, not even the killing of lady poets."

She went off, carrying the flat pizza carton. Carver and Rose waited, saying nothing. Rose began to fidget.

"She's been gone too long," she said. "More than five minutes."

"Yeah," Carver said, and clambered out.

He ran for the front door. Rose was behind him. She pulled a snub-nosed .38 revolver from her purse. He pushed random buttons, and the door buzzer went off. They went up the stairs.

Rose kept alert, her eyes scanning the foyer, the stairs, the landings. At the third floor they stopped.

"Oh, God," Rose said hoarsely.

Lorna Stokes lay on the scattered pizza carton. Her face was in the middle of the tomato-covered circle. Her eyes stared inches from the covering of sausage, pepperoni, and onions. A knife protruded from her back.

Carver cursed silently.

Cops. Cops. And more cops.

The police swarmed over the apartment building. Had anyone seen anything? Heard anything? There were eight apartments on four floors and the uniformed police knocked on all the tenants' doors looking for information. Apartment #6 was the apartment where Lorna Stokes was supposed to have delivered the pizza.

The elderly man and wife in that apartment denied ordering a pizza. Yes, they told detective Dan Gulden, they were positive. They were vegetarians, and if they had ordered a pizza it sure as hell wouldn't be with sausage and pepperoni. No sir!

Sergeant Ludlow and Detective Gulden interrogated Carver and Rose under the building's protective awning. Out of the rain.

"I don't know what to say," Ludlow said to Carver Bascombe. He shook his head dolefuly. "You're out of my sight for just a few fucking hours and another body crops up. Christ, you're some kinda grim reaper harvesting a wheat field. Every time I get a call from now on, I figure it's going to be you and another dead body."

Carver was silent.

Rose was silent. Otherwise she might rattle the ears off Ludlow. She handed the manila envelope to him and briefly told him the contents. The police could take it from there.

"Yeah, thanks, Rose," Ludlow said.

"What about Bovee?" Carver asked.

"We got an all-points out on him," Ludlow said. "He can't get too far. Leave this shit to us. Goddamn it, you finished your job for Laura and Raf, and he's pleased as hell. Laura is out of a jam, and it was a neat piece of work. I'll give you that. But from now on, leave the police work to us."

"What about Bovee?"

"What is this, a stuck record? We'll get him. Assuming Bovee knows who killed Hare and Stokes and Netsuke, or did it himself, then we'll nail him. It's only a matter of time."

"Yeah, I know," Carver said sarcastically.

"Yeah? Don't be smart," Ludlow said. "You don't know jack shit."

"Yes I do. I know Jack Shit. Don't I, Rose?"

"Of course. He's a sweetheart."

"One of nature's noblemen, old Jack. Getting a little ripe in his old age."

"Only when the wind is right," Rose added. "Descended from royalty, it's said. His royal anus."

"Yeah," Carver said, "the Shits of Europe. Descended from a long line of Shits."

"Stop it! Both of you!" Ludlow said. "Bascombe, you're

one stubborn bastard. Goddamn it, get your black ass outta here."

They left. Later, at the house, Rose led the way to the kitchen. She turned on the lights and put a kettle on to boil water.

"Ludlow!" was all Carver said, and laughed.

She laughed and Carver laughed, and he pulled off his shoes. Damn, he felt better.

"How about some nice tea?" Rose asked, barely able to get the words out between snickers.

"Bourbon," Carver said, and grinned.

Rose left the room. He wriggled his toes around and rubbed his feet over one another. Felt good. His feet burned and ached.

Rose returned, bottle in hand, and sat opposite and studied her partner. He seemed quite tired. But he chuckled again then broke out laughing.

"Now what, Boss?" she asked as she poured two shot glasses with Wild Turkey.

"Wait for a call," he answered.

"From who?"

"Bea Murphy," he said, and tossed back the ounce-and-a-half of whiskey. "I told her to take Royal Blue to a safe place. The less I knew where Royal was the better."

He picked up his shoes and went upstairs. He got out of his bloody clothes and changed into slacks and turtleneck shirt. He took a leather jacket and a snap-brim hat and returned to the kitchen. Rose had another bourbon ready for him.

"I've been trying to follow what's happened," Rose said, and shook her head, "but I don't see all of it."

"Neither do I," Carver admitted, and tossed back half the whiskey. "And we don't know the killer's motive. As for Bovee—it's greed, the old standby. Bovee needed cash to get his mansion out of hock—" He shook his head. "No, that's not right—"

"He'd already sold the house, Boss. He couldn't very well buy it back. Maybe he planned on settling down on some South Pacific island, let the world go by."

"I see that," Carver said, musing. "All right. Let's try

131

this . . . Bovee needed cash to save his computer company. He sold his mansion to do so. That company must mean a lot to him.'' He narrowed his eyes at Rose. ''What else do we know about JayVeeBee Enterprises?''

''Only what I got from the incorporating papers.''

''Who are the top officers?''

''I see where you're going. None of the poets were in the company.''

''Somebody named Lloyd?''

''No one by that name,'' Rose said, shaking her head. ''None of them. Not Geraldine Hare—and certainly not Laura. None. Anyway it doesn't answer why Geraldine Hare was murdered. Or Olive Dale or Lorna Stokes. Or even if they're connected.''

''I wonder. . . .'' Carver mused. ''Connections . . .''

''You thinking about Royal?''

''The lipstick on her mirror said she was next.''

''Yes—but she wasn't, was she?''

''No,'' Carver said, and ran a hand over the cleft in his chin. ''No . . . she wasn't.''

''You think it's possible she wrote that herself?''

He narrowed his eyes and said nothing. He didn't trust his own thoughts.

He reached for the kitchen phone and called Laura De Anza. After listening to her sincere thanks, he asked her if she had heard the news about Stokes.

''No, I haven't,'' Laura said, her voice apprehensive. ''What's happened?''

''I thought Raf might have heard from Ernie Ludlow.''

''No, and Raf's right here. What about . . . Lorna?''

''She was killed. Stabbed.''

A long moment hovered between the two telephones.

''Just like Geraldine,'' Laura said softly.

But not like Olive Dale, Carver thought, who was probably thrown from her balcony. And she wasn't shot to death like Clyde Netsuke. Carver thanked her and hung up. He finished the shot glass of Wild Turkey.

He called Gordon Dale's number.

''Yes, Mr. Bascombe?''

132

"One assignment down. Is your offer still open?"

"Indeed it is. I'll leave the results to you, Mr. Bascombe."

"Fine. We can discuss the details later."

"That's satisfactory. I have a feeling I'll rest easier tonight."

Carver hung up and stared into space.

"So," Rose mused, "A new client? You don't think the corporation angle is going anywhere?"

"I don't think so, no."

"Okay, then . . . right. Let's leave it to the cops. I'd say the killer's plan is totally ruined. And I say you can take the credit—or blame—for that. You can sleep good tonight, Boss. Good deeds for the day."

"God, Rose, you're really smearing the butter on thick and heavy. You must want that computer real bad."

Rose laughed and they talked over the same ground, trying different angles, but they came up with the same lack of answers.

The telephone rang.

"Hey, lad," Bea Murphy said, when Carver answered, "I've heard the six-o'clock news. You're getting right famous. Too bad about Stokes, though. You don't blame yourself, do you?"

"No," Carver said.

"Good. It was rather obvious, the killer called in an order for pizza, gave an address, and waited for Stokes to show up—and stabbed her. Right?"

"Yeah."

"Bloody well, I'm right. Okay—got a paper ready? Here's our new address and phone number."

Carver scribbled down the address, which was on Wawona Street, near Sigmund Stern Grove. He told Bea he'd be over in about half an hour. He took a Percodan tablet, washing it down with bourbon. He put a half-dozen tablets in his pocket, then gave Rose a copy of the address and telephone number. He went out to his parked car.

He scanned the street. All he saw were the trees, wet and

shiny and bending in the wind and rain. The running gutters gurgled. Cars parked on both sides. Nothing suspicious.

He throttled up the Chrysler and headed toward Twin Peaks. There was a method to this route: he didn't want a repeat of the tail job from his office to the motel to Netsuke's shop. He felt guilty about not being more alert.

The rain continued and slicked the streets. The wind battered at the Chrysler as he twisted it between the two landmark peaks, then down the other side, onto Portola Drive toward the Pacific Ocean.

Headlights followed him—but only for a few blocks, then turned off. A steady stream of traffic made its way down Portola Drive, and Carver kept his eye on the rearview mirror. The wind and rain lashed furiously as he turned at Sloat Boulevard. He steered the Chrysler onto Crestlake Drive, which took him around Sigmund Stern Grove.

He saw no one. He turned onto Wawona and parked close to the address Bea Murphy had given him.

The stucco house was two-story, with a view of the rustling, swaying eucalyptus trees in the grove. Carver had made the trip in less time than he had estimated. He spent time waiting in his car to see if any other auto turned onto the street from either end. Nothing. He was certain he hadn't been followed.

Before leaving the car, he checked his revolver. And made certain he had at least two full speed-loaders in his leather jacket.

NINETEEN

After letting him in, Bea told Carver the house belonged to a client of hers who was in Mexico, getting a dose of the sun.

Royal Blue was as fine-looking as ever. The tiredness and pain of the past few hours lifted from Carver. He could hardly keep his eyes off her. He could hardly keep his hands from her.

He didn't.

Carver took her in his arms, and she responded, pressing herself close to him. They kissed urgently, and then his mouth roamed gently over Royal's closed eyelids, her brow, her cheeks, and both sides of her mouth.

"Hey, Carver, lad," Bea Murphy said, getting his attention. "There's lots of time for that."

"Hello, Carver," Royal said, as she stepped back. She looked wide-eyed at him. "I don't know whether to be thrilled or embarrassed."

"I think I should look around the place," Carver said, fighting down his urge to grab her once again and kiss her hard. "I screwed up at the motel."

"Don't blame yourself for that," Bea Murphy said. "I've checked the house out several times. But—you don't look good, Carver."

"Have you heard about Lorna Stokes?" he asked.

135

They hadn't. Neither of them had felt much like watching the news or listening to the radio. Royal Blue had worked at her typewriter, and Bea made dinner.

"Excuse us, Royal," Carver said, and took Bea aside.

He told her about Netsuke—and about Bovee. He said little of his injuries and made no comment on getting shot at at the curio shop.

"It's getting bad, Carver," she said. "I think Rose is right—let's put everything on the table for the cops to chew over."

Carver said no and told her of Gordon Dale and JoAnne Stanton.

"There's more here," he said. "We've got to see it all the way."

"Don't leave her out of this, then. You can't protect her with silence. You can't shield her from information that's going to be on TV in a few hours. You must tell her. She has to know!"

"What's that, Carver?" Royal Blue asked, interrupting their talk. "What do I have to know?"

He realized Bea Murphy was right. He held his usual reserve in check as he narrated the events leading to Lorna Stokes's death.

Royal was appalled into silence. The house seemed to grow strangely quiet. The three sat in the living room, Carver in an easy chair, Bea and Royal on a sofa.

"That's awful," Royal said finally. "I would never have imagined such things. Stokes an addict, Bovee a wealthy man. Both living double lives. What the hell is going on, Carver?"

He stood and stretched. He did not answer her. There were no answers to give.

"Bea, I want to take a bath. I really need to soak. Think the owner would mind?"

"Sure, not at all," Bea replied. "Go to it, lad. I think you'll like the bathroom. I know damn well you will!"

Carver went up the stairs. The bathroom had as much space as a bedroom. A double-clamshell-sink vanity was inset into an alcove, which angled off the bathroom. Inside, redwood lined the curved walls. A large window over the immense tub gave a view of the grove of trees. The bathtub was a hot tub, with water jets bubbling along the sides.

The place had the scents of cedar and pine. Thick woolly towels hung from hand-carved rails. Carver placed several books of poetry on the generous edge of the tub, then undressed. He slid into the steaming water and let the whirling bubbles wriggle against his body. He barely filled a third of the tub.

He closed his eyes for a few minutes, then took one of the books and studied the poems of Harold Yoshima. Not the Haiku he was known for, but longer pieces in vers libre.

The hot water soothed him. He put Yoshima aside and studied Laura De Anza's poems, then Royal Blue's. For what it was worth he preferred Laura's. There was a great degree of warmth and humanity in her work. None of them seemed contrived.

The door opened—and Royal Blue stepped into the bathroom.

"Hi," she said.

He looked at her and realized why she had come to him. He put the book aside. Carver made no move to cover himself. She turned a dial on the wall, and the lighting lowered to a soft amber glow. Like candlelight.

Royal carried a large natural sponge and a bar of translucent heather-scented soap. She wet the sponge, then made a lather, and knelt down beside the tub.

"Lean forward," she asked.

She soaped his back, moving her hands slowly in large circles. Carver closed his eyes. She rinsed off the sponge, then rinsed his back, and repeated the lathering process. She moved the sponge over his shoulder, his neck, and down onto his chest.

He opened his eyes and looked at her; she didn't look at him. She smiled and continued soaping. He wondered if she thought he was too thin.

Not that it mattered, apparently. He watched her work.

"What's this scar?" she asked, her voice low, and rubbed at a puckered spot near Carver's ribs.

"Bullet," he said.

"And these?"

"Broken arm. Knife wound."

A sense of danger filtered through the steaming room. Hazard and fear became a part of sexual arousal between them. He wanted to say her name, but he feared breaking the spell. She handed the sponge to him and slowly undressed. Carver could not keep his eyes off her.

Her body was lean, with curves that seemed to flow in and out of secret places, their passage marked only with a gentle reminder of body hair. Royal stepped into the tub and lowered herself.

Carver leaned forward, his hands running over her moist skin. He kissed her mouth, and they clung to each other. The gentleness outpaced itself, and she clung to him, and he stroked her body, her arms, her face, her breasts.

Many minutes went by, and the bubbling water accompanied their touches, their kisses, and their silence.

"I need you," he said finally, the words tender and urgent.

"We need each other," Royal answered softly.

She moved under him, their upper bodies just under the waterline. Her eyes closed, she was mildly surprised to feel him inside her; she was barely aware of penetration. She felt filled, satiated.

They moved slowly, the hot water surging gently in a fabricated tide. She clung to him, gasping faintly, then heavily. His hands touched her in hollows, in folds, and the water lapped faster.

She was close—now, close to floating out of the window, out of the air, out into the night sky, the soft, rain-swept landscape, the world all of it out there and here and now all coming together.

She sighed and then shuddered.

"Poetry," she said finally.

Later, in bed, Carver lay in her arms, his eyes closed, feeling her breathing. Somehow he felt she wanted to talk, but the words were unnecessary.

Time passed, and she slept. He could not close his eyes.

Her touches, her body, the soft warmth of her desires swelled Carver's memory. The bedroom of fine carpet and watered-silk wall coverings seemed merely a gray pasture with limitless horizons.

Something intruded into his erotic thoughts.

He heard it but paid little attention to it. A sound. From downstairs. Then Carver's sense of self-preservation kicked into high gear.

Something had bumped hard. Like someone falling to the floor?

Carver rolled out of bed and removed his Colt Python from the holster hanging on a chair. He was naked, and he crouched on the floor. He waited to hear Bea Murphy call out that it was nothing. But there was no such call.

He heard footsteps coming cautiously up the stairs.

Carver went to the bed and slipped a hand over Royal Blue's mouth. She jerked awake.

"Shhh," he said. "Someone in the house."

She nodded, her eyes wide.

"Get on the floor."

Royal rolled off the bed, and Carver lay under the covers. He waited. He cocked the revolver. He heard Royal's intake of breath.

Then the footsteps paused. Outside the door. Carver breathed shallowly.

After long moments the door swung noiselessly into the bedroom. The soft hall light silhouetted the man. A big man. With a gun in his hand. Oddly Carver smelled a distinctive aroma of chocolate. The dark figure slowly reached up and leveled the gun at the bed.

The man cocked the hammer and muttered under his breath.

"Okay, nigger."

Carver shot him through the heart.

TWENTY

Royal Blue screamed.

"Easy," Carver said softly.

She stared into the darkness. She jerked her head in short arcs, her mouth open, her eyes wide.

Carver rolled naked from the bed and held her. Royal clung to him, her arms around his waist. The smell of his male closeness was strangely comforting.

He held her for long moments then slowly pushed himself away.

"I have to see what's happened to Bea Murphy," he explained, as she tried to hold on to him. "Please, stay here, Royal. Don't turn on any lights. Please."

"The man . . ."

"He's dead."

Royal whimpered, and Carver spoke a few comforting words. He hoped they were comforting.

"I've got to see if Bea Murphy is all right," he said finally.

In the dark he put on his pants and shirt, loosely strapped on the shoulder straps, and holstered the .357 revolver. At the door, a hallway light cast a dim amber glow. He looked at the dead man laying against the far wall from the bedroom door, his legs splayed across the hall. Blood spatters mottled the wall.

A fifteen-shot automatic pistol lay on the floor. Cocked. Carver didn't touch it. Let the cops check it out.

He looked at the man and recognized him. The man from the other night, the one in the red windbreaker, the big one. The one with chocolate breath.

Carver shook his head, puzzled. What the hell was going on? He was sure the two men had come from Lloyd, Holliday Kraft's manager (or pimp or whatever Kraft wanted to call him).

Was Lloyd (no last name) in this? Other than Holliday Kraft, what possible connection could there be between Lloyd and the murdered poets?

He stepped over the body and went downstairs.

Bea Murphy was in the foyer between the living room and dining room. She lay on her side, blood seeping into the carpet near her head. Carver checked his rage and knelt beside her. He tested the carotid artery in her neck—she was alive.

He turned her over. She had been struck in the temple, and the blood oozed from a deep laceration. In the kitchen he dampened a facecloth and wet her face. Bea blinked her eyes and slowly came around.

Far off in the distance he heard sirens wailing. It was a good bet that the neighbors had heard the shot and called the police.

In minutes the cops would be swarming all over.

Carver looked at the front door. Ajar and banging in the wind. How did the guy get in? More importantly how did the man know Carver was here? Or did someone know Bea and Royal were there?

No, the gunman was after Carver. He remembered the man's last words. Or was it possible—was he after Royal? Was the man merely waiting for Carver to show up? Then wait for the lights to go out and then enter the house?

Bea groaned.

"Hurts," she said.

"Yeah," he said, smiled at her, then went back upstairs.

Carver knelt and went through the man's pockets. He found a set of car keys and a half-eaten chocolate bar in one jacket pocket. In the other he found a leather pouch with a set of fine-steel door lock picks. A pro, he thought.

Carver shoved on his shoes and went downstairs. Bea Murphy was sitting up, wiping her head with the facecloth. Shakily she grinned at him.

"Be right back," Carver said.

She nodded and grimaced in pain.

The sirens grew louder.

He went outside. The wind had intensified. The trees bent and swayed, and the rain swept across the dark street in sheets. Across the street and down the block windows were lit, and a few people stood outside their front doors clutching their robes.

Six cars, including his own Chrysler, were parked on the house side of the street. About ten cars were parked on the other side. Bent to the wind and wet, Carver tried the dead man's car keys on the closest cars. On the fourth car, a late model Caddy, the door opened. He checked the glove compartment for a registration but found nothing.

The sirens were only blocks away now.

On the front floor was a small metal box—which he recognized. A direction finder.

Carver cursed, got out of the Cadillac and went to his Chrysler. He got a flashlight from the trunk and peered under the rear end. He found what he knew was going to be there: a signal transmitter. All the big man had to do was follow a homing beacon. Easy. He didn't have to tail him at all.

The homing beacon was held to the chassis by a powerful magnet. Carver pulled the transmitter off. He got inside the house as two black-and-whites pulled to the curb.

"I'll take care of this," Bea said at the door. "You get dressed, and Royal, too."

She turned on the porch light, and signaled to the police. The neighbors had congregated on the opposite sidewalk.

Upstairs Royal had turned on the lights. She was fully dressed in a skirt, blouse, and sweater.

"I'm all right," she said, as she saw the concerned look in his face. "I don't faint easy—but it is a bit nerve-racking to see a man . . . a man shot. Are you all right, Carver?"

"I'm all right," he answered, and put on his jacket. "The cops are downstairs."

"I heard. What are you going to tell them?"

"The truth."

"Will they—I mean, will they come up here?"

"They have to. Then they'll have the detectives here."

"What will they do to you?"

Carver shrugged. Royal Blue came to him and kissed him. The same strength of life and desire passed back and forth between them. He kissed her—then went downstairs.

Four uniformed cops were in the hall. Bea was displaying her head wound, and one of the cops looked at the outside door lock. One of the cops stiffened when he saw a black man coming down the stairs. Bea told him to cool it.

Royal followed Carver. The two younger cops looked at her appreciatively.

Carver introduced himself and showed the police his ID.

"Yeah, it's a valid license," one cop said, an older man, "but it's no license to kill. Where's the body?"

"Upstairs," Carver said.

"You got the weapon?" the older cop asked.

"Yes."

"Let's have it. Take it out easy-like. And hand it over."

Carver did as requested, with his left hand. One cop dropped it into a plastic bag. The older cop, who said he was Sergeant Vaughan, went up the stairs. Carver followed.

"Dead all right," Sergeant Vaughan said. "A magnum makes a real mess."

"It was self-defense," Carver said.

"Not for me to say," Sergeant Vaughan said, and shrugged.

Royal Blue turned as Carver and the sergeant returned. Carver had his hands behind him, and she heard the jingle of handcuffs.

TWENTY-ONE

Sergeant Ernie Ludlow sat in an easy chair and glowered at Carver Bascombe. To him, the house on Wawona was just some white man's show-off upper-middle-class house. Half the decorations looked like they'd been picked by some limp-wristed fag decorator.

He grumped and narrowed his eyes at Carver.

"You expect me to believe all this?" he asked.

Carver shrugged. He had given Ludlow the story almost as it happened. He had given him the direction-finder equipment.

Behind him the forensic team worked at photographing and fingerprinting. A police medic had bandaged Bea Murphy. Royal Blue sat quietly in a corner of the spacious living room; she kept her eyes averted from Carver and Ludlow. She looked through the dark windows to the wind bending the trees along the street.

Carver rubbed his wrists where the handcuffs had bitten into the flesh.

"We could put 'em back on," Ludlow said.

"I recognized the man," Carver said.

He said nothing more, since he had already identified the man as one of two who had beaten him.

"Yeah, so did I," Ludlow said. "Soon as I pinned him.

Name's Perry Dent. A hood. Got a sheet long and dirty as a whore's bed.''

"He works with another guy," Carver said.

"Yeah, usually. Lately it's been Sal Warsh. Both of them are in with Lloyd Naugall. A pool of sleaze and piles of scuzz butts.''

"He followed me here on a beacon.''

"Yeah, so you said," Ludlow said. "This homing-signal thing, you could've had it all along. You might've planted it, just to throw us off.''

"Why?'' Carver asked.

"Why not? You admit you took a mean beating the other night. You didn't report that of course. You never do. The same old shit. You know what's best, never mind the police. You might've been boiling to get even, know what I mean? You discover who the guys were and call them up—Dent and Warsh—and have them come here. Only one of them shows up. But you shoot him anyway.''

"You believe that?''

"Why not? It's as good as anything you've told me. Then you go out to Dent's car and plant the homing receiver and show us the sender gadget. You say it was under your car. You say.''

Carver knew Ludlow wasn't that stupid; the detective was merely frustrated and taking it out on him. He'd sit tight, but calm, cool. The cops would do their best to trace the direction-finder equipment, to trace where it had been purchased, and who had bought it.

At least the handcuffs were off. He had sat for over an hour with the metal clasps digging into him. He had sat calmly, not wriggling, so that the cuffs were just a nuisance. Then Ludlow had shown up. Ten minutes later the cuffs had been removed.

Bea Murphy sank into a chair and sighed. She gently rubbed the bulky bandage on her head. She looked at Carver and grinned. Then her attention was directed to the stairs as the body was being taken out in a body bag. The plastic creaked ominously as the two attendants manhandled it out the door.

A gust of wind caught the door and banged it against the wall. One of the attendants cursed. The wind howled and rain gusted into the hall. The windows in the house rattled, adding to the wind and rain noise. A policewoman wrestled the door shut.

"It's not a fit night out, yer honor," Murphy said to Ludlow. "We should all be in our trundle beds an' dreamin' of candy-floss meadows, gumdrop hills, candy-cane lanes, an' milk-shake lakes. A land of sugar an' spice. How about it, Sergeant, sir?"

"I like jack shit better," Ludlow said, and shook his head in disgust.

The medical examiner came over and spoke to him, and Ludlow nodded. Ludlow stood.

"Okay, yeah, Bascombe," Ludlow said, "we're goin' to seal off this house. It's officially a crime scene. All of you get out, and stay out. But stay within calling distance."

"You mean," Bea Murphy said, "I can't leave town?"

"You are not amusin', Murphy," Ludlow said. "I mean I want to know what you're doin' at all times."

"Well, tomorrow, sometime in the afternoon, I'll be goin' to a funeral. So will Carver, I imagine, and Miss Blue, too. That's out of town—in Colma, mortuary land. After that I cannot honestly say. It's in the ample lap of the gods."

"Whose funeral?"

"Geraldine Hare's funeral. I think you should be there, yer honor. I wouldn't be surprised if her killer showed up."

Sergeant Ludlow turned to Carver.

"Izzat right? You're goin' to this funeral?"

Carver sat quiet. Privately he wasn't sure he'd attend. He wanted time to think about the threads without a pattern. He wanted to talk to Raphael De Anza; Raf was a man who saw things in patterns. Between the two of them maybe they could unravel the warp and woof of the murders.

He wondered about Jack Bovee and Letitia. He asked Sergeant Ludlow if they had been picked up.

"Nah," Ludlow said. "Not yet. But he can't stay hid for long." He faced Royal Blue. "Lady, you've been silent. So hear this: Stay put in this town. I want to know where you are." He turned again to Carver. "Take her somewhere, Bascombe, I don't care where, but I want to know where. Not like last time. That motel, and now this house. You tell me where you are. All of you! Got that?"

"What did the medical examiner say?" Carver asked.

"Got that?" Ludlow demanded.

"What did he say?"

"You're such a smart ass, Bascombe. If I don't hear from you in an hour that you're out of the way, I'm going to a municipal judge I know, don't care if it is three in the morning, and I'm going to erase your license number off the state records. Maybe you got that, that time!"

"Ah, Sergeant, yer honor," Murphy said, "you're such a hard man. But I know that down deep, under that formidable exterior, is a soul totally lackin' in compassion. Think of this poor woman, yer honor, woke from a lovely sleep with a gunshot in her ear, and a dead man at her feet. An' her not knowin' whether the deadly deed was directed at her or at her friend. And you want to stand around accusin' us of wrongdoin'. Shame on a big man like you. What would your mother say?"

"Murphy, you are another smart ass," Ludlow replied. "And I wouldn't mind cancelin' your easy ride, either. Now the whole goddamn bunch of you get outta here."

"Yer honor, I think you're just burned because you know none of us had a thing to do with anything except self-defense."

"I know that! Get the hell out!"

Carver led Royal and Murphy out. They stood on the sidewalk, holding their clothes tight against the raging winds and rain. Murphy said she'd drive herself; Carver said he'd take Royal to his place. The two private detectives agreed to meet at the funeral.

Carver and Royal climbed into the Chrysler. He was worried about her, since she had said next to nothing for the past hour. As he parked in the driveway next to the house on Buchanan Street, Royal stared at him.

"Poetry is a fragile art," she said.

TWENTY-TWO

"Whose is this?" Royal Blue asked, and held up a delicate, lacy brassiere.

They were in Carver's bedroom. He looked at the object. Damn it, he was certain he had gotten rid of all of Claire Overton's clothes.

"A friend's," he said, and took the wisp of lingerie from Royal.

"It's all right," she said. Her tone was taut. "I know you didn't take a vow of celibacy. Is she anyone I should know about?"

"No," Carver said.

"Do you fall back on that monosyllable defense out of habit, or is it just a means of not answering."

Carver smiled. She was on the edge—yet she had handled her emotions well after the shooting. He knew she could keep it going.

"It's the way I am," he said.

"I know. I wouldn't want you any other way. I'm just trying to understand you."

He nodded. He wanted her to understand. She was the one woman in a long time who interested him.

Carver could cope with violence. His instinct, whatever it was, of needing to know, to follow a trail—that was part of himself.

Years past, he had often misunderstood his motives. It took a while before he had accepted himself. He was a hunter.

Carver brightened like a nova when in the middle of a chase. He felt white-hot, stimulated when challenged with a universe of questions that demanded an infinity of answers.

"I should be more . . ." Royal said slowly and hesitantly ". . . I don't know—somehow more—insecure perhaps. And terrified. Yet, somehow—I don't feel—as shattered—

"Violence doesn't frighten me that much," she continued. "I grew up in a housing project. There were drug dealers in every stairwell. I saw a few people—boys and girls—dead. Dead before they were seventeen. One before she was twelve." Royal trembled and held herself. "It toughens you. In one way. But . . . you never get over it. I'd bury myself in a book, not think about it."

"I understand," he said.

How could he be both violent and tender? she thought. But he wasn't violent; the word meant furious, forcible, wild, fierce, raging, ungovernable. Carver was cool, calm, studied, compassionate.

He was complex; he pursued goals she could never understand; he was a solace, a comforter. Yet somehow she knew he could not sacrifice his life to the demons of terror and revenge.

Carver took her in his arms, and she felt the alarms and fears of the night fall slowly away. Royal felt comfort and warmth sift through her body.

"I dont want my bra to be a trophy," she whispered.

He pressed his lips to her throat and tasted the hollow there.

"No," he whispered.

She arched her neck and felt a release of fears, her apprehensions dissolved by a glowing yearning.

"How do you like your eggs?" Royal asked.

The aroma of French-roast coffee filled the spacious kitchen. Carver glanced up from the morning newspaper.

"Any way," he said. "Make it the way you like. How about you, Rose?"

"I'll tell you again," Rose Weinbaum said, "there is no way to spoil an egg. Although a poached egg was a terrible thing to do to an egg, not worth bothering with. Make them scrambled, Royal."

Royal cracked several more eggs into the frying pan. She poured a cup of coffee for Rose. She stirred the eggs, folded the potatoes, and looked over her shoulder at Carver.

"Is it in the paper?" she asked.

"Page five," he said. "Next to a discount-TV-store ad. No names mentioned, pending the further outcome of the police investigation."

She slid plates of scrambled eggs, diced ham, and hash browns onto the table. Rose thanked her as Royal joined them. Carver read aloud the story on page five. He had a second cup of coffee.

He had slept well, despite being up past three in the morning. But sleeping with Royal, any male would sleep well. He looked at his watch: almost ten-thirty.

The phone rang, and it was Mike Tettsui.

"You better turn on the TV, Carver," Tettsui said. "It's Claire's talk show."

Carver went into his office and turned on the television set. Rose and Royal followed him. Claire Overton was in the midst of a conversation with a policewoman.

. . . but this private detective seems to be in the middle of a real mystery. The homicide department seems to be following on his heels, while Carver Bascombe runs amok in a series of murders. Why hasn't the department acknowledged the fact that a killer is trying to wipe out the female poets in the poetry group?"

"I can't answer for all detectives," the policewoman said, "because it's against department policy to speculate on an ongoing investigation. If this private detective is withholding information from the police—"

"Oh, he is," Claire Overton said. "He hasn't told the department all he knows about the poet Lorna Stokes, a cocaine addict, and owner of a local pizza shop."

"We're investigating that," the policewoman said.

"Of course. But what about the other poet, Jack Bovee, who has also been leading a double life—I'm sure the police would like to know about that. And then there is the possibility of a strange man named Lloyd, who seems to be in the thick of the plot."

"We really don't feel it's right to speculate—"

"Oh, I know, I'm speaking out of turn, but it's one of the chances we take for our audiences—"

The morning audience clapped enthusiastically.

"—and then there is the lady poet, the one who wrote the naughty poem about orgasm—"

The audience gasped. A pleased gasp.

"—Bascombe isn't sure she isn't mixed up in it."

Carver stood transfixed. Claire had done it again! But how? Where was she getting her information?

"Carver!" Royal Blue said. "Is that true? You think I'm mixed up in this?"

TWENTY-THREE

"Goddamn it!" Carver exploded.

How did Claire know so much?

Only one answer!

He turned to Rose.

"She's had our place bugged," he said.

"Yes," Rose said. "It's the only explanation."

Royal Blue looked from one to the other.

"You mean," she said, "she's had some kind of wiretap put in here?"

"Sure," Rose said. "But she doesn't know how to do that herself—"

"She had someone do it," Carver finished.

"Carver!" Royal said. "You didn't answer—"

"No, Royal, I don't suspect you. I may have sometime back—"

"You!" she said.

"Easy, Royal," Rose said. "Everyone is suspect in a situation like this. Everyone. It's the nature of the job."

At his desk Carver took out the keys Claire had returned. He tried them in the front door. They wouldn't turn the lock or the bolt.

"Rose, Rose, I've been stupid," Carver said. "She put one over on me. Me." He felt foolish and witless. "She gave me another set of keys. Kept the house keys I gave her. Then hired some expert who came in and put in a wiretap."

Rose unscrewed the mouthpiece of her telephone. She found nothing.

As Royal watched, oddly fascinated, Carver went to a cabinet and took out an electronic sweep. He spent the next half hour carefully going over the walls, the desks, the phones, the chairs, bookcases, everything.

The first bug transmitter was under the kneehole in his desk. The second was concealed behind an Ellsworth Kelly framed print in Rose's office. The third bug was tucked under the banister newel post on the stairway.

Another was in the kitchen, across the top of the frame of the pantry door. Carver avoided Royal's eyes; he felt like a fool. He should've guessed Claire would stoop to this.

And he wasn't surprised she had.

Carver went up the stairs, using the sweep. Royal and Rose followed. After an hour they had found only one other transmitter: in the lamp on the night table next to his bed.

"They could hear everything?" Royal asked.

"Yeah," he answered, almost under his breath.

Was she ashamed? Embarrassed? He looked at her. No—

she seemed composed. But someone had listened to their lovemaking. Yeah, someone had come in, planted the bugs, knowing it was an invasion of privacy.

Claire must have had a good laugh as she listened to the playback. Or did she? Maybe she'd been furious. That was more like it, he decided. The emotional combination of her lust for a good story and her jealousy would account for her exposé on the air.

"What are you going to do?" Royal asked, as they returned to Carver's office.

"I'm going to see her," he said, and tossed the tiny microphones into the cabinet, along with the electronic sweep.

"Think you got them all?" Rose asked.

"Yeah," Carver said, sounding more positive than he felt.

At least he had got five of the little demons. Later, when he had more time, when he was calmer, he would sweep the house again. Top to bottom.

Some of those electronics guys were wizards. Some of the bugs might've been decoys, with others hidden in more ingenious places.

The police had the Colt Python he had used on Perry Dent, the intruder. He opened the file cabinet's top drawer and took out another .357 Python, which was in a leather-and-sheepskin case. He wouldn't wear it—not in the mood he was in. He might shoot Claire Overton.

"Easy with that," Rose said. "Claire has you by the shorts. The damage has been done, and we're lucky we don't have reporters camped in our front yard. Thank God for this rain!"

"I'll think of something," he said. "Can you take care of Royal?"

"Oh, no," Royal said, "I'm going with you."

Carver shook his head. There was no way she was going with him. Not when he was going to see a former lover. He didn't want to be looking over his shoulder to be certain that Royal was safe, out of danger.

He explained this as well as he could.

"Carver," Rose said, "don't worry about it." She turned

to Royal. "You come with me. Find out what we do around here. When we know what we're doing, that is."

"Check Yoshima's background," Carver said. "I had a thread but couldn't put it together before. But now I remember a connection. Yoshima said he worked for a computer firm—East Wind Process in Silicon Valley. And Bovee owned a computer firm, JayVeeBee Enterprises. That was one connection—"

"And they were coeditors," Rose added, "so there seems to be a tie-in of some kind. I'll see what I can find. I'll research those two companies. And I still have research on Holliday Kraft to do."

They agreed to meet at Geraldine Hare's funeral.

"The sooner we get out of here," Rose said, "the better. I can smell reporters swooping down on us."

Carver went first, checking the street for TV vans or cars with reporters. He was in luck. Nothing.

The rain beat down furiously, driving leaves into the gutter, choking the overflow grates. Small branches clattered down the street, beating a twiggy tattoo to the overture of wind and rain.

He locked the revolver in the box in the Chrysler's trunk. He drove off, and Rose and Royal left several minutes later.

Hurrying storm clouds and driving rain obscured the view of the bay from the glass elevator outside the broadcast-building tower. Carver Bascombe didn't look at it as he rode up.

He barely paused at the door to Claire Overton's offices. The decor was gray carpet spread to the walls, high-tech chrome-and-black glass tables and curvilinear fabric-covered chairs. A middle-aged blond secretary sat behind a white laminated desk.

"May I ask your business—" she started to say.

Carver stalked on by and went into Claire's private office. The secretary made loud noises, but he ignored them. He closed the door.

Claire Overton looked up from her work sheets.

"How'd you like the show?" she asked. "My, Carver dear, you do seem upset."

"You had my house wiretapped."

"Yes, I did. When Rose was at the library. I had several of the electronics staff here do the job; they owed me."

"I pulled the bugs out."

"So what? What can you do about it? You're going to sue? You're going to serve legal documents against me? Go ahead, Carver! You'll look like a fucking fool after the newspapers and media get through with our story."

"*We* don't have a story."

"Not anymore. That's positive! I heard the tapes from last night. You and Royal Blue—very sexy stuff. I heard you quite clearly. And she thinks you're full of poetry? I know what you're full of! So you see, Carver dear, I was right. You were going to dump me—"

"Stay out of my business," Carver said bluntly and hard.

"Of course, lover. I've had my fun. As I said, I can smell the winds. If I were you, I'd take your lumps and like it. You're not in the kind of business where you can afford to wash dirty linen in public."

Carver said nothing. He knew she was right—or half-right. But he couldn't undo his throwing her out of the house. Claire's revenge was complete. As complete as she wanted.

Dust to dust—or rather mud to mud.

The mourners and clergy at Geraldine Hare's grave numbered about thirty.

A canvas canopy had been erected over the site. Against wild winds the canvas cracked and whacked like a clipper ship going around the Horn.

At a distance, Carver Bascombe watched the final burial rites for the murdered poet. He wore a snap-brimmed hat and a serviceable, warm overcoat. He huddled under a drooping willow, its branches and small leaves cascading back and forth like a green octopus writhing its way under the sea.

For the past forty-five minutes about a dozen poets had read eulogies composed to Hare's life and art. The ceremony wasn't over, but a male figure detached itself from the group and walked to the weeping willow. The man was wrapped in a thick muffler, hat, and raincoat.

"I thought it was you," Raphael De Anza said to Carver. "Still playing the outsider."

Carver hunched himself against the cold and wind. He pulled up the collar of the overcoat around his ears.

"Ernie Ludlow told me," De Anza said, "that they went looking for Holliday Kraft. Nobody there in her apartment. Apparently cleared out."

"What about Jack Bovee and Harold Yoshima?"

"Ludlow and Gulden went to Bovee's apartment. But he wasn't there. Is that interesting or is it?"

"Interesting," Carver said.

"Then Ludlow and Gulden went to Harold Yoshima's apartment, and he hasn't been seen around for the past twenty-four hours."

"Try where he worked?"

"Oh, sure, but guess what—he doesn't work there."

"Wait a minute—" Carver began.

"No—he's not an employee. He owns the company."

"What?"

"Another one with a lot of lies to answer for. And the cops haven't seen hide nor hair of Jack Bovee. Or that woman with him—"

"Letitia," Carver supplied.

"Yeah, her. Her name's Letitia Ormandy, we found out. Captain Callahan thought maybe Yoshima or Kraft or any of them might show up here—but so far, nothing. And in this weather, I don't think they will."

"What about the direction finder?"

"It's only been a few hours, *compadre*, and they aren't telling me everything—after all, with Laura innocent beyond doubt, they've got to start over. And in this weather—"

"I bleed for them," Carver said.

"Yeah, amigo, me, too. Anyway, they've located the place where those direction-finder gadgets were originally bought. An electronics retailer down the peninsula in Burlingame. The store's records don't say much about the buyer, but it was only about six months ago. They thought the buyer was a company in Silicon Valley. One of those electronics outfits, but the owner of the store couldn't remember which one.''

"Did they suggest JayVeeBee Enterprises?"

"Bovee's company? No, they didn't. I'll suggest it. Give them more rope."

"Don't burn your bridges, Raf," Carver said.

"I know when to fold my cards. Homicide is my department, too—when they let me work a good case. Right now Captain Callahan is watching me real close. After all, I almost had his job."

"All right. Keep me informed if you can."

"*Sí*, and you do the same. We're in this together."

They shook hands, and by the time De Anza had returned, the mourners were drifting away. Rose and Royal saw him and started to head for him. A woman hurried her footsteps and reached Carver first.

"I have to talk to you," she said.

Carver didn't recognize her at first. A designer label umbrella hid much of her face. She wore a stylish rain hat, an expensive fur-trimmed coat, gloves, and fur-lined boots. She had good looks, the kind seen in expensive beauty salons. But even hidden under expertly applied makeup, the spray of freckles identified her.

"Hello, Letitia," Carver said, and gripped her gloved right hand. "Got a paperweight hidden in those clothes?"

"Don't be funny, Bascombe," she said. "This is serious. You shot Jack, you know."

"But he isn't dead."

"No thanks to you. I bandaged him up. Mostly the bullet went through skin. But he wants to see you."

"Now?"

"No, of course not, not now! With all the cops around here? Even I could smell them. No, he wants to meet you tonight. You know about the big poetry reading, where all the local poets are coming together—"

"I know about it," Carver said. "On board the *Verdugo*."

"Yes, the old ferryboat. Okay, Jack told me to tell you

he'd be there. And he's willing to talk to only you. No cops! Understand? Absolutely no cops.''

"All right. But just so Bovee knows, tell him I know he's a liar. What he says had better be damn convincing.''

"He says you won't be disappointed.''

With that, Letitia Ormandy turned and hurried away, umbrella bent into the wind.

Another figure detached itself from the parade of umbrellas moving away from the grave site. Carver shook his head; he was very popular for some reason. The figure was a woman—and he recognized JoAnne Stanton as she drew close.

"Thank you, Mr. Bascombe,'' Stanton said, and pumped his hand. "Gordon told me you were going to do what you could for us.''

"I made no promises, JoAnne.''

"We understand—but I know you'll do your best. Somehow I think your best is worth five times anyone else's efforts. Thank you again.''

She walked away toward the parking lot. Carver watched her get into a BMW and drive off. She certainly didn't ask what his best consisted of. He wasn't sure he could tell her.

Carver then joined the march of bobbing umbrellas. He met Rose and Royal, and he held Royal close. Under her umbrella they kissed. She made elfin pleasure sounds.

Damn it was good to see her, he thought. Rose and Royal furled their umbrellas, and the three got in Rose's car.

"God, it's wet and cold,'' Royal said. "It was a nice service. Gerry would've appreciated it. I wish I had composed something. She wasn't such a terrible person to know.''

Carver nodded and asked Rose what they had found out in the past few hours.

"We've been chasing company ghosts, but I think we found something about Yoshima—''

"He owns East Wind Process,'' Carver said.

"What the hell do you need me for?'' Rose said. "You're doing all right just standing under a tree.''

"All right, Rose.''

"All right is right. Yoshima owns this electronics firm.

Deals mostly with the software end of computers. Yoshima's company is almost belly-up."

"Financial problems?" Carver asked.

"The worst. The kind even a competitor wouldn't try for an unfriendly takeover."

"How'd you get this?"

"I checked the amount of business JayVeeBee Enterprises had done, and a couple of companies—at least until last year—did a lot of transactions with JayVeeBee. It was a hunch, but we checked those companies' corporate structures and found Harold Yoshima was the president of East Wind Process."

"One step more," Carver said, and told them about Letitia asking him to meet Jack Bovee at the poetry reading.

"I was supposed to be there," Royal said. "I should be, too."

"It might be dangerous," Carver said. "I'd feel better if you stayed with Rose."

He got out and headed for his Chrysler. A man under a black umbrella moved alongside Carver.

"Not that way, Bascombe," the man said, and jabbed a snub-nosed revolver into Carver's neck.

The man cocked the weapon. A cold chill, colder than rain, trickled up Carver's spine.

Carver recognized him. One of the two men who had beat him up outside Harold Yoshima's apartment house the other night. The partner of the big chocolate eater he had killed. Ludlow had told him the big man, Perry Dent, usually worked with a guy—Sal Warsh, Ludlow had said. Both worked for Lloyd. Holliday Kraft's Lloyd. Lloyd Naugall was his name, Ludlow had said.

"Hello, Sal," Carver said.

"Okay, so you know me. This .38 is loaded and cocked. Just stay still. . . ."

Sal Warsh searched Carver and found only the cassette recorder in his shirt pocket. He removed it.

"Okay, black boy," Warsh said, "see that big limo over there?"

The limousine was black and looked much like part of the entourage of cars from the mortuary.

"Yeah," Carver said.

"Okay, move your ass over there."

TWENTY-FOUR

Carver was pushed into the rear seat of the limo. He sat next to a slim, dapper man dressed in a custom-tailored suit, highly polished shoes, and matching gray-silk pocket kerchief and necktie.

The limousine pulled out of the cemetery parking lot and turned north on Hillside Boulevard.

"Bascombe," the well-dressed man said, "I'm Lloyd Naugall."

"How's Holliday?" Carver asked.

Naugall's large, liquid blue eyes seemed saddened. His stubby, manicured fingers were laced together over his midriff. He turned to Sal Warsh, who sat next to the driver.

"He's clean," Warsh said, "except for this."

He handed over the tape recorder, and Naugall held it as though it were some kind of soiled underwear. He ejected the micro-cassette, electrically lowered the dark window, and flipped out the cassette. He handed back the recorder to Sal Warsh.

"You killed my man," Naugall said.

Carver was silent. He didn't like the phony-sad tone of Naugall's voice.

"You're probably right," Naugall said. "It's better not to say a word. There's not much defense for the deed."

He raised his hand and slapped Carver across the face.

The warehouse was somewhere in the Visitacion Valley district. The rain beat on the metal roof, and the cavernous interior acted as an echo chamber. The sound was constant, faintly drumming. The air was cold. Vapor escaped from the mouths of Sal Warsh, Lloyd Naugall, and the limo chauffeur. Holliday Kraft was also there, wrapped in furs.

Carver Bascombe was tied to a chair. A single overhead light cast a nebulous ring around him.

"Now we'll talk," Naugall said.

"You won't like this," Holliday said to Carver.

"Why did you kill Perry?" Naugall asked.

"He was going to shoot me," Carver said. "Or the lady with me."

"I find that hard to believe," Naugall said. "That wasn't his job in my organization."

"Then someone else paid him."

"My associates and employees don't take free-lance assignments."

"I find that hard to believe."

"Don't mock me, Bascombe. Holliday has told me about you. Her estimation of you was on the money. Are you a hard man? I don't think so. In my experience, nobody is ever hard enough."

"How are you, Holliday?" Carver asked.

"In excellent health, Carver. However, Lloyd's been inconvenienced. He's had to make other arrangements for me."

"Which means—what?"

"Not what you think. I—and other associates of the corporation—have been relocated."

"I don't like cops," Naugall said, "and I especially don't like them messing into my business. And you've caused them to be most intrusive. However, that is sometimes the cost of operation. Let's get back to Perry."

"Let's."

"Tell me the circumstances. And tell it straight. I don't mind telling you I have sterling sources in the police department. I've read the detective's report on the shooting. Now the cops assumed the statement you gave them was true—but I don't. So you had best be quite convincing."

Carver gave a brief, accurate account of the shooting of Perry Dent.

"Well done," Naugall said when Carver was finished. "Quite concise. However, I don't believe you. Let me tell you what I think really happened—you lured Perry there, as an act of revenge for the beating he gave you. I don't say you intended to kill him—"

"Yeah, the hell he didn't," Sal Warsh interrupted. "This black pussy didn't have the balls to take us on together. He wanted to beat the shit out of Perry first—and then he was going to go after me. Like I said, Mr. Naugall."

"I believe those are the facts," Naugall said to Carver. "You didn't expect Perry to come armed. After you saw he had a gun, you killed him, before he had a chance to use it."

"No," Carver said.

Holliday chuckled and turned away, as though violence bored her.

"Then you planted the gun next to him. And told that lie to the police that Dent came in with gun drawn."

Carver understood why Naugall didn't believe him—because Naugall assumed Sal Warsh spoke the truth.

"I don't like you, Bascombe," Lloyd Naugall said, and slapped Carver across the face.

He hit Carver in the face with his fist. Right hand—then with the left hand. Carver tried to roll with the punches, but it was useless. By the fourth punch to the face his lips were split, and blood spilled from his mouth.

"Wait . . ." he managed to get out.

Naugall paused, his fist cocked shoulder-high.

"Listen to me, listen," Carver said thickly, lisping the s's.

"Okay, Bascombe, I'm listening."

"How did the lady PI get her head bashed?"

162

"Rigged," Naugall said. "Or it happened earlier in an unrelated accident."

"You got him there, Mr. Naugall," Warsh said.

"For the sake of argument," Carver said, and spit blood, "assume I'm telling the truth."

Naugall nodded, his eyes narrowed.

"Assume I shot Dent in self-defense—then he had to be working for someone else—all right?"

"I'm still listening."

"Then since . . ." Carver's mind raced, ". . . Dent usually worked with Warsh—that's right, isn't it?"

"Yes—so?"

"Then it might make sense that Warsh knows Dent took on a free-lance assignment. Assume he knows Dent was hired to kill me. Maybe Warsh was offered the same job—but turned it down."

Naugall absorbed what Carver said and turned to Sal Warsh.

"Well . . . How about that, Sal?"

"It's bullshit, Mr. Naugall!" Warsh said. "Perry wouldn't go behind your back. Me either!"

"I don't know, Sal," Naugall said, musing. "About three months ago—you and Perry asked for a raise. I turned you down. I explained we might reconsider the request after we generate more income."

"But that don't mean we took on anything outside—we know better—we knew you wouldn't like it."

Lloyd Naugall turned to Carver and shrugged.

"Well, there you have it, Bascombe. It's your word against Sal's."

"You've got me helpless and tied up," Carver said. "You might get me to admit anything. Let's turn it around—let's put Warsh in my place and work him over—then see what he says."

"Gee, Lloyd," Holliday said to Naugall, "that sounds like fun."

"You nigger sonuvabitch!" Sal Warsh yelled and pulled a gun. "You got a fuckin' nerve!"

He whacked Carver across the head. And again.

Through a haze Carver heard Naugall yell to Warsh to stop and heard a struggling commotion. A third voice yelled. Probably Holliday's. Carver didn't much care; he slipped into a blackness that spread like a Rorschach blot in his mind and swallowed him up.

Down, down, into gloom—then gray light. In Carver's mind a vague image flickered—a word—

Guile . . . The word—and something else—something about hands. A motion of a hand—

And somewhere in the obsidian depths he saw the face of the killer of Geraldine Hare and Lorna Stokes. Everything fell into place!

He opened his eyes in surprise. God! A tell!

He was on his back on the concrete floor of the warehouse. Blurry-eyed he saw Lloyd Naugall, Holliday Kraft, and the chauffeur. He coughed and spit out blood. He could move. He was no longer tied to the chair.

He tried to get up, but his body ached with intense pain. What was it he remembered? Damn it! It was important!

Oh, yeah! A tell!

Carver concentrated. He lay his cheek on the chilly concrete and closed his eyes. Remember—remember! Let the subconscious rise!

Harold Yoshima! He had an unconscious habit, a tell. Whenever he was telling a lie, he stroked his throat, letting his fingers trail onto the necktie he wore.

What had Yoshima said whenever he stroked his throat?

Yoshima had said he wanted to help Laura De Anza. He'd stroked his throat and tie.

Yoshima had said he thought Laura capable of murder. He stroked the tie.

He had said he knew nothing about the killing of Geraldine Hare. Stroke, stroke.

Lies! Lies!

Lloyd Naugall turned and saw Carver was conscious.

"Are you all right, Bascombe?"

Carver groaned and sat up.

"Sal knocked you out," Naugall explained, "and I can only assume he thought I believed you. He ran off. Thereby guaranteeing his guilty knowledge, as far as I'm concerned. As you assumed, he probably knew all about Perry's freelance assignment. I suppose I should have paid him more; Perry would probably still be alive."

"You're a lucky man, Carver," Holliday Kraft said.

She gestured and the chauffeur helped Carver to his feet and put him in the limousine. Naugall and Holliday sat next to him. She opened the backseat liquor bar and poured a snifter of brandy and gave it to Carver.

They drove out of the warehouse. Naugall gave orders to the chauffeur to return to the cemetery.

"You can get your car there," Naugall said to Carver.

Carver nodded and drank the brandy. His ribs grated in his chest, his face was swollen and bruised. His head felt like it would fall apart in two halves.

"You're welcome," Naugall said, with a tinge of sarcasm. "You're effusive thanks are enough. Actually, I'm glad you were telling the truth. I need loyal employees, and it's so difficult to determine which are most reliable."

"Yes, Lloyd," Holliday said. "It's not as if we can advertise in the want ads."

"Too bad," Carver said.

"I believe," Naugall said, "I've instilled more respect in my associates than I had ever intended." He chuckled and sipped his brandy. "I'm not a killer, Bascombe. I'm in the pleasure business, not the death business."

"Poor Sal," Holliday said. "He looked funny—running for his life."

"Truly believing, I suppose," Naugall added, "that I would hunt him down and liquidate him." He refilled Carver's snifter. "I think I'll hire college graduates from this time forward. I presume I'll have to test them for contemporary mores and beliefs. Do you think that process would be of value in my line of trade?"

TWENTY-FIVE

Carver pulled into the driveway next to the Victorian house. He locked the car and went inside. Rose looked up from her typing.

"God, Carver, you look terrible!"

"Again," he said.

"As bad as before, Boss. Keep this up and you're going to run out of flesh and clothes."

She helped him out of his jacket and shirt and planted him in his desk chair. From her office she brought the first-aid kit.

She tried a humorous aside about having to take the state's RN test. He didn't laugh or chuckle.

"You're worse off than I thought," Rose said.

"Where's Royal?"

"Upstairs. Sleeping. She's worn out. What happened this time?"

He told her, then added:

"I know who the killer is."

Rose paused, bandage in one hand, scissors in the other.

"I have an idea about that, too. Let me guess?"

Carver nodded.

"It's Harold Yoshima."

"Yeah—how did you figure it, Rose?"

"It was a process of elimination. Since we both agreed

166

Laura didn't do it, I assumed it was one of the poets at the dinner meeting that night. Later, Stokes was killed. That left only Holliday Kraft, Royal Blue, Jack Bovee, and Yoshima."

"Yeah—go on," Carver urged. He had gone through a similar thought process.

"You said there was a computer connection between Bovee and Yoshima. They were both in that business. But so was Royal Blue."

"Yes," Carver said. "I worried about that. But she was an employee of a computer company—and she alibied no one for that night."

"Right, but Yoshima and Bovee alibied each other—"

"Yeah, but Bovee had to elaborate the alibi, with that walk down to Fisherman's Wharf."

"And in the past couple hours," Rose continued, "I've heard from Herb Randall at Tan-ta-Mount Logic about Yoshima's computer company. East Wind Process. Guess how Yoshima got the computer company?"

"Don't tease, Rose."

"He inherited it. From his late wife." She paused. "Randall told me the story. And to double-check, I looked it up in newspaper files. About ten years ago, this young woman, whose family owned a computer company, married a young Japanese poet, Harold Yoshima. Then less than two years later, she's dead from—and get this—a drunken fall from a balcony."

"Like Olive Beem Dale."

"Yes. Yoshima apparently knows a good thing when it works. But there was no suspicion of wrongdoing, since he was at a party with a good friend—"

"Jack Bovee," Carver said.

"You got it. Mr. Bovee alibied Yoshima. So Yoshima inherited the company. But Herb Randall says Yoshima couldn't keep it out of the red ink. The business went down slowly, but was definitely in deep financial trouble."

Carver nodded and winced as Rose pressed a bandage to his head.

He told Rose his ideas on Perry Dent. Since the beating took place on the same street where Yoshima lived, it was probable that he saw the beating. Yoshima must have followed the two men, found out where they lived, and later approached them with a contract to hit Carver.

"There's more yet," Rose said. "Frank Needlemeier called back. He's cagey and suspicious but is willing to talk with you. Herb Randall says Needlemeier is some kind of computer whiz. I think Needlemeier knows something."

"Did he give a hint?"

"No, but I suggested he meet you at Specs' at six o'clock."

"Good thinking, Rose. Not much chance of anyone we know seeing us. And he agreed?"

"Yes, most emphatically. Herb Randall gave you good marks."

Carver nodded and thought.

Damn it, the case was turning. He was after Yoshima, and probably Bovee, and—something else. He'd have to let De Anza know about this. The question was—when would he tell him.

"We're coming down the last road," Carver said. "I need information to open up Bovee—so I'm definitely going to talk with Needlemeier—before I meet Bovee at the poetry reading."

He put in a call to both Mike Tettsui and Bea Murphy. They agreed to met him at Specs' 12 Adler bar. From there they'd go to the *Verdugo*, the ferryboat where the poetry conference would take place.

He shoved himself into warm slacks, holster, sweater, then a jacket. The night was going to be cold. He made several other calls. Then put on an old overcoat and a snap-brim hat.

"I can feel it," he said. "Setting the stalking goat."

"I have to trust you," Frank Needlemeier said.

Carver nodded and studied the man—under five-foot-seven, with broad shoulders, broad brow, and intense green eyes behind air-force-styled sunglasses. Carver suspected the green eyes were from colored contact lenses.

Perhaps Needlemeier thought the sunglasses would protect his identity. The patrons of 12 Adler Place stared at him, as though he were some bourgeois oddity. Needlemeier paid no attention; his eyes were on Carver Bascombe.

"Herb Randall said I could trust you," he said. He twisted his fingers together as though warming them. "I don't want to get in the middle of an ugly lawsuit. If I lost such a lawsuit, I'd probably never work in this industry again. No one would trust me. Ever. Understand?"

"Yes, Frank. Our conversation is confidential."

"Okay, good. Are you familiar with the theory and mathematics of topology?"

"I've heard of it," Carver said, then paused, thinking. "It has to do with the study of continuous surfaces, inside and out—like a Möbius strip or a Klein bottle."

"That's it," he said, and ran his hands through the air as if they could describe a shape. "You see, it was my concept, my idea of using topological math. But of course it is a complex analytical system."

Specs came over and they ordered a pair of hot brandies.

"My mathematical specialty," Needlemeier continued, "has been a study of topologic surfaces. Now the Möbius strip is any length of any material with the outer strip twisted, turned over one-hundred-and-eighty degrees, and joined to itself, so that it becomes at once its own inside and outside." His fingers traced a complex maneuver, one hand over the other. "It is without thickness, and has no dimensionality, since it has a single surface. Mathematically it has no end, no beginning."

Specs set the brandies on the table, and Carver asked for a repeat order. Specs said sure, and out of Needlemeier's line of sight, jerked his head to the bar counter. Carver nodded a quarter-inch; he had already seen Murphy and Tettsui sitting at opposite ends of the bar.

"Naturally, topologically speaking," Needlemeier said, "it can be any topological round surface or a kind of cube." He made a square shape in the air with his hands. "Sort of a cube. Composed of layers of topological strips."

"Wait, just a moment, Needlemeier," Carver said, shaking his head. "You've left me way behind. I don't understand what topology has to do with anything."

"You don't?" Needlemeier asked. "Didn't I tell you?"

"Whatever it is, you didn't."

"It's about microchips, Mr. Bascombe." He put a finger alongside his mouth. "I didn't say anything about chips?"

"No," Carver said, still pleasant and patient.

"I'm talking about topological math applied to the design of microchips and circuitry. I've always been fascinated in the paradoxes of topology. Sort of a mathematical optical illusion. This would be infinite power, within the finite confines of set-point logic." He flicked his fingers at the universe. "Retrieval time and search time reduced to nanoseconds. A stretch in logic circuitry that can reduce the size of a super-computer to a bread box."

Specs came with two more brandies. Frank Needlemeier thanked the man for being so prompt. Needlemeier drank eagerly, Carver cautiously.

"Imagine, Mr. Bascombe—a processing time with a potentiality of sixty-eight megabytes of data per nanosecond. A microchip design capable of such storage and recovery speeds in a minute size would be worth the entire computer business gross for a year."

"I'll take your word for it," Carver said.

"That's just the chip-and-circuit formulation. Think of the other hardware components. The information floppy discs for instance. Perhaps we might come up with a new kind of hard disc. A different shape than we've seen before." His hands weaved a peculiar twisted shape over the empty brandy glasses. "A topological mathematical shape. It would take enormous finances to R & D—you know what that is?"

"Research and Development."

"Fine, fine, Mr. Bascombe, we understand each other. Such development would take a new look at computer-programming mathematics. The research time involved would take years. But I'm speaking in the past tense. Such a breakthrough has occurred."

He smiled at Carver, started on the second brandy, and returned to his narration.

"Yes, it was six months ago. The whole thing has been developed in a cooperative effort by several of the leading

Silicon Valley firms working secretly as partners. But there was a concern over security. Despite our best efforts, the finished equations and designs have probably been stolen."

"You don't know?"

"Not for sure, Mr. Bascombe. The original designs are safe in a vault. But there have been rumors—terrifying rumors—that they have been copied—photographed. The chip design could be sold to any competing company. The thief could realize perhaps tens of millions from such a sale."

"And you think—this person—stole the plans?"

"Or had someone do it for him. We have no proof—"

"Let me say a name—Harold Yoshima."

Frank Needlemeier's mouth dropped open.

"My God! Randall said you were good—Yes! Yoshima."

"You have no proof Yoshima stole it."

"No, just suspicions," Needlemeier said. He finished the second glass and ordered a third. "You see—he—came to me about four or five months ago and offered me a huge sum to sell him the plans. He didn't say it in so many words, of course. I didn't admit there was such a thing. And he didn't come right out and say he wanted to buy the plans. All innuendo, if you know what I mean. But it was easy to read between the lines. Mostly he was sounding me out. You see . . . it was common knowledge his company was going broke. Then suddenly he acquired an infusion of capital. I suspect it was a down payment from an outside computer firm for the chip design. Possibly a foreign company. More than likely a Japanese corporation."

"But you can't prove it," Carver said.

"No, I cannot. That's why I was most suspicious when you called."

Carver believed Needlemeier's suppositions. He believed Yoshima had stolen the designs. Which left questions: How was he going to get the designs out of the country? And when? Had he already accomplished that task?

Another thought struck him. He believed he knew why Lorna Stokes was murdered. And Geraldine Hare. And Olive Beem Dale.

"If you get those designs back, Mr. Bascombe," Needlemeier said, "I'd be particularly grateful. The company I work for would be incredibly grateful. They'd know they could stay in business, their designs protected. I know you would be well paid."

Carver nodded, deep in thought. He was positive the designs were still in the city, or close by.

"What do you plan to do?" Needlemeier asked. "About what I've told you."

"I'm going to a poetry reading."

"Oh."

"I think I'll run into Yoshima there."

"Ah, I see. Then what will you do, Mr. Bascombe?"

"Take him—and get those designs back to you."

TWENTY-SIX

The night was punctuated with the lonely bonging buoys in the bay.

Rain pelted the wharf planking, and the dark wood glistened. The wharf was at the far end of the Hyde Street Pier. The ancient ferryboat *Verdugo* was tied up next to several vessels of similar historical interest.

Crowds converged on the *Verdugo* as a bobbing tide of umbrellas. Spirits were high.

Several TV-station vans were parked close to the gangplank. Bright quartz lights illuminated the people surging on board. Nearby, a TV reporter rehearsed her opening speech, which would be seen on the eleven o'clock news.

Carver went on board. He slapped the rain from his hat. Hands in his overcoat pockets, he circulated among the poetry lovers and the poets.

Several reporters were interviewing the more renowned ones. A chamber-music quartet played Haydn in one passenger deck area. Up front, under the wheelhouse, a three-piece rock band (one guitar, synthesizer keyboard, and drums) rattled the windows.

Near the side-wheels, by the refreshment stand, on the stairwells, anywhere there was space, poets gave readings. The music mingled with the verbal cadences.

Carver recognized Lawrence Ferlinghetti, Robert Hass, and Joyce Jenkins. Many of the poets were young. Some were shy, others were boisterous, and others were a mix of dramatic, gentle, arrogant, or sincere to the point of agony. All were in love with words.

The mingling crowds went from poet to poet, sometimes staying and listening appreciatively. Others sampled. A few nervy ones asked for autographs.

Beer and hard liquor flowed. Paper cups went from hand to lip. Words went from mouth to ear. Poetry went from mind to mind. Occasionally a poet was rewarded with a round of applause.

The shy poets cast their eyes down, as a gentle smile flickered. The proud, arrogant poets received their accolades as their due. The angry ones furrowed their brows, as though the audience didn't appreciate the compositions enough, or for the wrong reasons.

A gray-whiskered poet gestured dramatically, making his points, and sneaked looks at the six listeners for appreciative interest on their faces.

Carver Bascombe located a setup bar. He ordered a Wild Turkey but settled for the house bourbon.

Bea Murphy went from group to group. She listened for a few minutes, then moved on, circling the perimeter of the ferryboat about every twenty minutes.

Eventually Carver spotted Letitia Ormandy. She was

dressed for the cold in a thick fur coat and a fur hat. She was well made up, but again her freckles gave her away. She came over to Carver.

"Jack will talk with you when this is all over. When he can see that no one has followed you. Only until then."

"Where?"

"I'll tell you when and where, Bascombe."

"You don't like me much."

"No, not much. Jack and me, we could've had a fine life. But you had to come along and fuck things up."

"Bovee did that to himself."

"Bullshit, Bascombe—"

"Nice alliteration," Carver said.

"Bull! Jack never committed any crimes. He's sick with worry, and he's afraid."

"Yeah. He just lied to protect Harold Yoshima."

"You can't prove that by me. Anyway, we just wait. I'll be around."

She moved away. Carver didn't follow her; Murphy had seen her and Carver gave a nod in Letitia's direction. Murphy trailed her.

Then Carver stiffened. Royal Blue came into view. She wore a fashionable designer raincoat, which she hung next to a folding card table. She put a plastic bag and attaché case on the table.

What the hell was she up to? Carver asked himself. Was she going to read? He went over to her, and Royal was excited to see him.

She kissed him, and he found himself kissing her back. Royal had the ability to push his emotions to the hilt.

"Rose told me you'd be here," she said. "I couldn't keep away, not for something like this. It isn't often that people get a chance to hear as many poets as this." She paused, and the look on her face clouded. "Besides, I couldn't stay at your place, as nice as Rose is. I kept seeing the face of the dead man—does that sound crazy?"

"No, Royal, it doesn't."

"The look on his face—the blood—" She shuddered. "I don't think I'll ever forget it. I had to get my mind off it.

174

This conference was a perfect escape. I needed human contact."

"This could be dangerous, Royal," he said, and held her close.

"With so many people around? What could happen, really?" She drew back for a moment and looked oddly at him. "You're wearing a gun. I felt it—"

"Never mind," he said.

"Do you think seriously that Jack Bovee would do something crazy in all this crowd?"

"It's not Bovee I'm worried about. And how did you—"

"Rose and I are becoming quite good friends," she offered as a way of explanation.

"All right," he said, giving in to the situation. "I'll be over by that bar."

"Are you offering me a drink?"

"No."

"God, what a grouch."

Royal smiled and returned to her table. She set up a half-dozen folding chairs. She urged people passing by to sit and listen. Nobody paid much attention until she displayed books of her orgasm poem and a desk tag with her name on it.

A crowd soon gathered, and she read. Carver watched a minute, then scanned the crowd. Despite the damp, the cold, the crowds, the people were having a good time.

Bea Murphy came by, and Carver told her to keep an eye on Royal. She nodded and stayed within eyeball distance of Royal.

Several hours went by. The bars had continuous patrons. Poets extolled their art. Reporters came and went. Carver's feet hurt. He desperately wanted to take off his shoes and give his toes a good rubbing.

By ten o'clock the program was over. The poetry lovers left the ferryboat. Poets folded up their tables. The bartenders put away their wares.

Letitia Ormandy came to Carver. She had a hand in the pocket of her coat, and Carver figured she had a handgun there.

"It's okay now. It's time," she said, and jerked her coat pocket at him. "He's upstairs."

Carver went ahead and knew Murphy and Tettsui watched from the shadows. Letitia climbed the narrow, interior stairs that led to the wheelhouse. As they reached the next deck, a man pushed Carver aside, and Carver sprawled. The man grabbed Letitia by her coat and slammed her head against the wall. She slumped to the decking.

Carver jumped to his feet and went for his .357.

"Don't, Bascombe," the man said in a harsh whisper.

He held an automatic pistol. In the dim light cast by the wheelhouse bulbs Carver saw the elongated barrel. A silencer. Carver recognized the man. Sal Warsh.

"You fucked things up," Warsh said. "For me—and you killed Dent. That's all for you, Bascombe."

TWENTY-SEVEN

Carver whirled and flung himself along the deck. He slid along the boards in a spray and disappeared into the darkness. Sal Warsh fired several silenced shots into the blackness. The sounds were like large beetles crushed underfoot.

Carver rolled fast several times, then scampered upright. His feet slithered on the wet deck boards. He scanned the gloom. To the front was the upper-prow deck, lined with rows of passenger benches. No cover there!

To his left was the port side, with a narrow walkway along

the length of the *Verdugo*. The starboard was the same. In the middle was the wheelhouse, with wide glass windows streaked with rain. The wheelhouse would be a death trap. Not much use as cover.

Another shot coughed, and Carver heard the air crack as the bullet snapped past. In a crouch he moved along the deck, keeping close to the shadows of the wheelhouse. He looked up; the deck was roofed over, as modest protection against the elements for the nineteenth-century passengers.

He leaped, caught the lip of the roof, and swung himself up. Had Warsh heard the movement? He lay on the roof for a long moment. He felt as if his back had broken. Certainly his ribs screeched in protest.

For illumination tall stanchions with low-wattage bulbs were spaced along the railings. In the rain they only cast a highlight on the deck railings and on the nearest benches. The rest was blackness.

The wheelhouse lights shed minimum illumination across the deck. Carver slowly raised himself. Laying down, he'd be too easy a target if Sal Warsh climbed onto the roof. He swayed against the buffeting wind and rain. He moved carefully, worried his footstep sounds would carry below.

A plan formed in his mind. He worked his way to the port side, in a direct line with the dim light cast from the wheelhouse. He squatted near the edge, his hands outspread, ready. Patience, patience.

He couldn't take a chance on using his Python. He might drop it into the water. Carver waited with wind-driven rain slashing across his eyes.

Minutes went by—and then underneath, a shadow blotted out the wheelhouse lights. He swung out, caught the edge of the roof gutter, (Oh, damn! it was wet and slippery!) and held on. He let his weight carry him out over the water. Then under the roof in an arc.

His feet together. He wanted maximum impact—if he had planned right.

He struck Sal Warsh in the face. The man flew back, his eyes blank, his arms out. Warsh slammed into the wheelhouse. Carver heard—rather than saw—the silenced pistol clatter across the deck.

Carver hit the deck awkwardly. He had only been concerned with striking at Warsh. He sprawled, slithering, tumbling on the wet boards. He pushed to his feet, and Sal Warsh scrambled upright.

Warsh wiped blood from his nose and faced Carver in a crouch. He threw himself at Carver, grasping both the detective's hands. They braced against each other, breathing hard, their eyes contracted to slits.

Carver jammed a knee into Warsh's crotch. The man's eyes bulged. Carver backed off and hit him in the jaw. Warsh went back, sidestepping, then they were on each other, grunting, heaving.

Warsh slammed an elbow into Carver's face. And shoved. Carver stumbled back. Warsh whirled, scanned the deck, made a dash—and scooped up the silenced automatic.

Panting, Carver faced him. Lit by the light from the wheelhouse, Warsh leveled the pistol—and Carver saw a glittering object arc through the air. A stiletto buried itself in Warsh's upper arm.

The gunman dropped his pistol.

"Get him!" Bea Murphy yelled.

Carver stepped in and slapped his hands against Warsh's ears. The man screwed his face in pain and grabbed his head. Carver dropped him with a chop to the neck and a straight-finger jab to the sternum.

Sal Warsh lay still on the deck.

Bea Murphy plucked the knife from Warsh's arm.

"Late, but not too late," she said as she wiped the knife clean. She slipped it back into its sheath behind her neck.

"And we," Sergeant Ludlow said, coming onto the scene, "found this dame—"

With Detective Dan Gulden and a bunch of cops, Ludlow held Letitia Ormandy in one beefy paw. Letitia was in handcuffs. She cursed Carver and Ludlow.

"What a sweetheart," Ludlow said sarcastically. He shoved Letitia into the arms of a policewoman. "Take the bitch away."

Ludlow barked more orders, and the other cops took Sal Warsh away. He turned stoically to Carver and Bea Murphy.

Carver watched Letitia and Sal Warsh taken away. Poor woman, he thought. She was plain scared, not the shooting kind. He thanked Bea for the knife work. They both gave a brief statement to Ludlow and Gulden.

"We waited," Ludlow said, "until we figured you and Bovee would've been deep in gabbing. Then we were going to take him. Sorry we didn't catch on sooner about Warsh. So where is he?"

"Bovee?" Carver said. "You probably scared him off."

Ludlow and Gulden gave orders, and the cops searched the ferryboat, but found no trace of Bovee. He had vanished. And Letitia was silent.

Wearing his snap-brim hat again, Carver went down to the lower deck. He made sure that Bea Murphy took Royal Blue away. Royal was concerned about him, and it took a few minutes of cautious explanation to get her to leave.

He walked off the ferryboat. Carver found a spot on the wharf in deep shadow—a wet, black shelter of boxes, gear housing, and cable spools. He waited patiently, the rain dripping from his coat and hat. Long after the last police car had gone, he returned to the lower deck and sat on a bench. His eyes were accustomed to the gloom.

Out of the corner of his eye he caught a movement from across the wharf, where the *Eureka* was moored. A figure moved cautiously through the shadows, taking his time. Finally the figure climbed silently up a ladder on the side of the *Verdugo*.

Carver eased the .357 Python out of his shoulder holster. He put the gun by his side.

From above, a gruff chuckle came from the gloom.

"You won't need that, bro'."

Carver shrugged.

"Well, come on up," Jack Bovee said in a low voice. "We'll talk."

TWENTY-EIGHT

Against the wet cold, Jack Bovee had wrapped himself in a heavy dark coat. A hat was pulled low across his eyes. The poet was a bare silhouette, his dark skin blending with the night, the rain, the shadows. He stood outside the wheelhouse, under the shelter of the overhang.

Bovee nodded as Carver came up the stairs.

They faced each other, holding their balance as the old ferryboat rocked with the tide and the growing, howling wind.

Carver was tired, exhausted. He hurt! Pain continued to thrust and jab in Carver Bascombe's body. His ribs grated, his shoulders ached, and his face felt as though it had been scrubbed against a cheese grater.

"I want Yoshima," Carver said.

"Yeah, well, bro', so do I. He's left me holding the shitty end of the stick. But how did you figure it was him?"

At that moment he loathed Bovee for his indifferent, casual attitude. Carver held the gun by his side; he knew the black barrel was difficult to see, but he kept it pressed close to his body.

"The computer connection, Jack," Carver said, "that was the first piece. And you were friends, coeditors of the poetry anthology."

"I can see how that stood out. The rest of it, bro', now that must've taken some fancy figuring."

"I finally tumbled to Yosh's tell."

"His what?"

"A tell. When Yoshima lies he strokes his throat and his tie. A habit he was probably unaware of."

"Jesus," Bovee said.

"Then you lied about your alibi. The two of you matched up a story, but you embellished yours. A creative act that made me suspicious."

"I just didn't believe he'd killed Geraldine Hare. I want you to believe that. It was too bizarre to believe."

"Lorna Stokes was his true target," Carver said. "Yoshima had no reason to kill Olive Dale, or Hare. It was Stokes he wanted—"

"Bascombe, she blackmailed Yosh. A lot of the downpayment money for stealing the microchip design went to Lorna. She knew he had stolen those designs, and she needed money."

"For her cocaine habit—"

"Yeah? A junkie? I didn't know . . ."

"And Lorna wanted to pay off the mortgage on her pizza franchise. Yoshima figured he could disguise her death by killing other female poets. Get the cops to look for some kind of serial killer nut. Throw the cops off on a false trail."

"He's the nut," Bovee said. "And he's dangerous. I didn't think so at first."

"Neither did I," Carver admitted. "But I read his poetry, and I saw that much of it was about guile—and deception—and deceit. That and the other factors—"

"Yeah, Bascombe, a nut case. The night his wife died, he asked me—real friendly like, but worried—to alibi him. He told me he just didn't want to be investigated. He swore his wife's death was an accident. I believed him."

"What about the death of Olive Beem Dale?"

"That's when I began to think it was too much of a coincidence. I began to believe it a few days ago. The killing of Geraldine Hare was so—so unexpected—"

"How'd he do it, if you were together and you weren't aware of it?"

"I figured it out, sort of. I guess he saw Gerry coming down the other street from across the parking lot—he said to keep an eye out, that he had to take a whiz, couldn't hold it any longer. He went into the lot behind some cars. He was in shadow, and I couldn't see him—"

"Then he stabbed Geraldine Hare—"

"Yeah, I figured that—and then he joined me, faking like he was zipping his pants. Later, when I realized—I was in shock, I swear. I didn't think he'd done any of it. Then I knew I was part of it—and in too deep—"

"You trashed Royal Blue's apartment," Carver said.

"Yeah, yeah, I did. I admit it. He arranged it while she was with him that night. A good alibi for him, and he had me by the balls. I was involved, he said. It was more of his crazy plan to make the cops think there was a weirdo trying to kill female poets. It was crazy! He was nuts! Before that, I swear to God, Bascombe, before that I didn't know. You've got to believe me."

"Doesn't matter. You have to convince the police, and a jury."

"What can I do, Bascombe? I need help."

"Let me take you to the cops. Make a statement, Jack."

"Damn!" Bovee said, and shook his head. "I never wanted anyone to die. Not to save Yosh's company. Believe me, I don't hold human life that cheap. I'd sold the mansion. The money was there to bail my company out—even his company. If he'd waited, I think we might've both come out of it."

"But he probably didn't believe you'd help him," Carver said. "So he stole the microchip design."

"Yes, yes, damn him," Bovee said, his words barely a whisper. "He told me! Damn! I was out of my mind. Then he told me Stokes was blackmailing him. That's when he planned for me to trash Blue's apartment. He figured Stokes had to die without any suspicion falling on him."

"How did she find out he'd stolen the designs?"

"I don't know. Yosh never said."

"Where is he, Jack?" Carver asked.

"I swear, Bascombe, I don't know—"

"How were the designs going to be sold?"

"He never told me, I swear—"

"Who was the buyer?"

"Some Japanese company he had contact with—"

The first bullet buried itself in the wood paneling less than four inches from Carver's head. He went down for cover. The second bullet dug into the deck a foot from his face.

The third shot threw Bovee against the rail. Bovee cried out and he went over. His gun drawn, Carver crouched and ran to help. Another shot drove him back.

He figured the bullets were probably coming from the *Eureka*, the ferry on the other side of the wharf. Someone—Yoshima!—wanted him dead!

Bovee was in the water, struggling, his hands flailing. He looked up, eyes frenzied.

Carver lowered himself, holding on with one hand. Another shot cracked through the night. He ducked. He tried again to reach Bovee—he called out his name—and Bovee twisted in the water. The man's arms were raised helplessly.

Another shot banged into the deck near Carver's feet. He threw himself into the shadows and fired in the direction of the *Eureka*.

He looked into the water. Blood stained the surface. The ferryboat surged in the tide, and the pile railings thrust dangerously close. Carver saw them and realized he might get crushed.

The *Verdugo* rolled against the pilings. Jack Bovee screamed and sank out of sight.

TWENTY-NINE

The last of the police had left the *Verdugo*. The harbor police had found no trace of Jack Bovee.

In Specs' 12 Adler Place Museum and Café, Carver sat with Raphael De Anza. Carver worked at a double shot of Wild Turkey. De Anza nursed a hot brandy.

"Had to be Yoshima," De Anza said, and rolled a half-dozen rifle-cartridge casings on the tabletop. "We found these on the upper deck of the *Eureka*. It's got to be a good two hundred feet. And trying to shoot in this wind and rain . . . he probably used a night scope on a sniper rifle—"

"Thank God for that wind and rain," Carver said. "He missed. Probably shot Bovee by accident."

"I think he's some kind of sociopath. A real nut case."

"I want him," Carver said harshly. "And I want those chip designs."

"Where is he? And those plans? Ludlow searched Yoshima's apartment. Yoshima left everything behind. The only things missing were his books, his computer discs—he even left the computer—and he took every scrap of paper in the place."

"Raf, he can get another computer. But the discs—he'd need those. Wherever he was going." Carver thought for a long moment. "Did they find anything of the poetry anthology?"

"Nothing, according to Ludlow. It was probably on the floppies."

Carver shook his head and reflected. The man didn't just drop off the world. He had to go into hiding somewhere.

"How big would the microchip plans be?" De Anza asked.

"I'll be damned," Carver said. "I never asked Needlemeier."

"Call him," De Anza ordered.

Carver put in a call and came back in a few minutes.

"Needlemeier says the circuit designs based on his equations would be large sheets, like blueprints. But he said if he were Yoshima, he'd take them down in size—"

"Microdots!"

"Needlemeier says dozens of them. That's the way he'd do it. Raf, is there any place where Yoshima might've had the photoreducing done?"

"Maybe in his plant at East Wind Process. Ludlow went down there today when he couldn't find Yoshima at his apartment. I went along unofficially. He had disappeared. Just like Holliday Kraft. Which made us suspicious of both of them. He wasn't at the plant, which was all but closed down—but I remember seeing a small audiovisual department there."

"That's a possibility. Let's go."

De Anza agreed. In Carver's car they drove south for an hour to the area known as Silicon Valley. The windshield wipers flicked at the rain bombarding the car.

Carver told De Anza many of his assumptions and the paths he had deduced that led him to figure Harold Yoshima was the killer. He skillfully excised any speculation about the relationship between Olive Dale, Gordon Dale, JoAnne Stanton, and Geraldine Hare.

He was engrossed in the narration, watching his words. The Highway 101 traffic flowed around them. He didn't notice a car following behind.

The East Wind Process company plant was on a side street off the Bayshore Freeway. The building was one story, of cinder block, steel, and glass. The building was almost empty, with only a few lights on at that time of night.

They parked in the small lot. The other car, its headlights out, pulled into the side street and parked.

"Somebody's working late," De Anza said, as they stood outside the glass entrance."

"Yoshima?" Carver suggested.

"One way to find out," De Anza said, and went through the entrance.

"Hey!" a young man said. He stood by a desk littered with papers. "You can't come in here."

De Anza showed the man his badge. The man said his name was Adams and told them Yoshima wasn't there. Adams said he was just clearing out his desk.

"And I don't know when Mr. Yoshima will be back," Adams said dispiritedly.

"Why not?" Carver demanded.

"Because he came in here yesterday, and said the plant was going to shut down until further notice—" Adams choked on the words, and scratched at a meager mustache. "It's not going to be easy to find another job. And I've got a wife and kid depending on me."

"Did he do anything out of the ordinary?"

"Just the usual. He spent a lot of time in the photo room. He's been working on a book. A mock-up of the real thing. The photo room has a drafting table."

Adams pointed out the photo room, and De Anza and Carver went in. The room was small, but there was an excellent enlarger that could also have been used as a reducer. On the drafting table they found several sheets of dry-copied papers—poems that were probably going to be used in the anthology.

Yeah, it made sense, Carver thought. It figured. Yoshima was going to have the poetry anthology dummy mock-up sent to Japan.

And he bet himself the dummy had another purpose—to hold the microdots. Maybe. Was Yoshima taking the mock-up dummy pages to Japan by air? If so, then he'd be over the Pacific Ocean already. With no way to stop him!

THIRTY

No, Yoshima wasn't flying across the Pacific, Carver realized. Yoshima had one fear—flying. No way the poet was going to take an airplane to Japan. There was only one other way across the ocean. By boat. A freighter, perhaps. Or maybe a pleasure cruise liner.

"What'd you find?" De Anza asked.

Carver explained his assumptions.

"Then there's a chance we'll get him," De Anza said excitedly. He paused, thinking. "Or then again he might have mailed the dummy."

"I doubt that, Raf. Would you trust something that valuable to the mails? Especially overseas mail?"

"Probably not. Yeah. But—he could have faxed it. Get there in minutes." He paused, thoughtful. "No, no he wouldn't—the microdots wouldn't have reproduced worth a damn. They'd just be black spots."

"I'm betting he's hand-carrying it across the Pacific."

"Well, he can't have gotten too far," De Anza said. "Let's find out what ships are sailing to Japan tonight or tomorrow."

"He might've driven to Long Beach in Los Angeles. There might be a ship leaving there, and he could drive it in six or seven hours."

"Easy enough to check," De Anza said.

They went into Harold Yoshima's darkened office, and De Anza made his first call to the Port Authority.

Carver looked around the office. He looked on Yoshima's desk, at a year-planning notebook. The current day had been circled with a red pen. And a time—12:00. P.M.? A.M.?

"Okay, no way Yoshima's bound for Long Beach. There isn't any boat bound for Japan for a couple of days."

"What about—"

"The guy's checking. Just hold it, Carver."

The two men waited, and finally the voice on the other end spoke. De Anza listened intently.

"This has to be it!" De Anza said. "There's a freighter bound for Japan tonight. The *Shika Maru*; leaving from India Dock Basin. The harbor master says it's scheduled to leave at midnight. Tonight."

"That's it," Carver said. He looked at his watch. "We can drive back in less than an hour. We could just make it."

"I'll try to have the harbor master stop the sailing schedule. And I'll alert the harbor police."

"Better have Ludlow meet us there," Carver added.

They ran out, wished young Adams luck, and jumped into the Chrysler. They drove quickly out of the lot and headed for Highway 101 north.

The other car followed closely behind.

THIRTY-ONE

A mad, slashing rain drenched the night. An occasional glare of lightning threw the wharf and the *Shika Maru* into stark black and white. The wharf asphalt crazily reflected the harbor lights of the India Dock Basin docking area.

Like a great metal wall, the ship towered over the docking sheds. A sprinkle of work lights outlined the masts, the bridge, the radio and radar antenna. The cables squeaked in the wind. Rain cascaded from the bridge to the deck. Water sloshed down the ropes and rained heavily into the water below.

Lightning flashed and thunder rolled over the bay some seconds later.

The *Shika Maru* was an obsolete ocean-going freighter of some ten thousand tons. The ship took up much of the four-hundred-foot pier. Thick ropes tied to bollards held it to the land. The tide barely moved the ship; the waterline was up to the top of the red mark on the hull. The ship was fully loaded and ready for sailing.

Sergeant Ludlow huddled next to the pier sheds. Carver and De Anza drove up and parked.

"Anything?" De Anza shouted at Sergeant Ludlow.

"Nah," Ludlow said, just as loudly. "Except for some ship's officers, nobody's come on board. Not since we got here. Maybe a half hour ago."

"He must be on board," Carver said.

The wind abated momentarily.

"You may be right, Bascombe," Ludlow shouted, "but we can't go on board."

Carver shrugged. Rain dripped from his hat brim, making glittering prisms passing across his vision of the *Shika Maru*.

"Ernie, it's our case," De Anza said. "As much as it is yours."

"Yeah," Ludlow replied unconvincingly. "The chief of detectives is going to shoot my ass off for havin' you around."

A captain from the harbor police walked down the gangplank. He came up to them.

"Sorry, Sergeant, but there's nothing we can do. Your man might be on board, but the captain of the ship is the final authority. He says the *Shika Maru* is a freighter and does not carry passengers. Without a warrant—you're out of luck."

"We don't have enough hard evidence," Ludlow said. "Not enough to get a warrant."

"When does she sail?" Carver asked.

"In less than thirty minutes," the harbor police captain replied. "We can't delay that sailing unless we have a reason." The harbor police captain paused. "There isn't anything we can do."

"Shit!" Ludlow said, and began arguing legal technicalities.

Carver edged himself away from the trio of police. Let them bicker over the legal fine points; he knew the law as well. Harold Yoshima had to be on board. Had to!

He stood in the rain and made up his mind. Against the wind, he staggered to the gangplank. He mounted it. His overcoat was drenched. He heard his name called but paid no attention.

He wanted Harold Yoshima. Alive. The poet was going to face a judge and jury.

He made his way along the deck to where he thought the officers' cabins would be. He unlatched a steel door and entered a well-lit hallway. He closed the door and the sound of the storm was instantly sealed off. The silence was eery.

He shivered from the abrupt change of temperatures: cold outside, warm inside. Or perhaps he shivered from the dire stillness.

So far he had seen no one. Not a ship's officer, nor a seaman. Carver jammed his hat into his overcoat pocket then took off the coat and slung it over one shoulder. The hall was deserted. On either side was a row of cabin doors.

Cautiously he opened each cabin door. They were officers' cabins. In minutes he had completed his search. No one was in any of the cabins. Carver figured they were all busy getting the ship ready to sail. None of the cabins had given indications Harold Yoshima occupied one.

Or maybe Yoshima wasn't on board. Maybe he and De Anza had misinterpreted all the clues that had led to the *Shika Maru*. But Carver didn't believe it. He brushed his doubts away.

He made his way along the passageway. He encountered one Japanese man, apparently a steward, who glanced at him curiously. The steward hesitated but did not stop. And he didn't block Carver. The man quickened his pace and just before turning a corner, glanced back at Carver.

Why hadn't the man asked him why he was there? Or ask what he wanted? After all, a black man on board a Japanese freighter?

He followed the steward but stayed out of sight. The man hurried down long corridors then entered a glassed-in salon. Carver pressed himself flat against the wall, hidden from view by the salon's wide door panels.

There were groups of officers at small tables and at the bar. Carver counted nine officers.

And there was Harold Yoshima—sitting at a table with a drink in his hands.

THIRTY-TWO

Yoshima was not alone. A white-suited officer in a braided cap sat opposite, with a small sake cup in front of him. A bottle of sake and a bottle of whiskey shared the center of the table. Yoshima and the officer seemed to be friends.

The steward went to Yoshima, bowed, and gestured, apparently telling Yoshima something. Carver figured it had to be about himself.

Yoshima nodded, the steward bowed again, moved off, and Yoshima got up. He spoke to the officer, who nodded; then Yoshima went out a far door that led to the deck.

Carver went back down the corridor, then out a door. He saw Yoshima crossing the deck to a door under the bridge. Captain's quarters, Carver figured. First officer. Maybe second officer as well. Of course . . . Yoshima was probably sharing the cabin with that officer or had a senior officer's cabin to himself.

He followed, stepped through the steel doorway—and Yoshima drove a vicious karate chop at Carver's neck.

The overcoat over his shoulder took the brunt of the chop. Carver threw himself back—tripped over the steel doorsill, and hit the rain-pelted deck.

He rolled, and Yoshima landed on him. Carver thrust the overcoat into Yoshima's face. They rolled around on the wet deck, each trying to get a hand on the other's throat.

A roar of wind and rain drenched the two men. A lightning glare caught them frozen, like an enormous strobe light.

Tangled together, they slammed into some steps. The steel stairway led to the bridge. Carver shook himself loose. He managed to get to his feet. Yoshima tossed the coat aside. In a crouch he faced Carver.

Yoshima gestured "come to me," and grinned.

The man's hair was a matted, damp mass. Yoshima wiped his face. He never took his eyes off Carver. He circled him. Carver waited for Yoshima to make the first move. They said nothing.

Carver cursed silently. Yoshima was unarmed, but he had his hands. Probably enough! He remade the vow: he wanted Harold Yoshima alive.

Lightning flashed. The radiant light bathed the ship in an instant of blue-white light.

Thunder bellowed across the heavens.

From the bridge Carver heard shouted commands. The wind whipped across the deck and carried the sounds of steel doors opening and closing. Out of the corner of his eyes, Carver saw sailors moving across the deck. Their figures were dim in the rain. Then a shudder went through the decks; Carver felt it through his feet. The *Shika Maru* was getting ready to sail.

Carver drew his .357 Python. He watched Yoshima's face. The man's expression was neutral. But guarded. Carver carefully, deliberately opened the cylinder. He pushed the ejection rod a fraction. The cartridges were glints of light in the lightning.

He let the cartridges slip back into the cylinder. He closed the weapon. He bent to the rain-swept deck. Yoshima's eyes followed the movement. Carver watched his expression— and pushed the revolver between them.

He stood and looked at Yoshima's eyes. Would the man go for the challenge?

THIRTY-THREE

Was Yoshima going to go for it? Did he think this was a trick? A move to get him to reach for it? Damn right! Then Carver would kick the man's head in. But not to kill him.

A small smile crossed Harold Yoshima's face. He moved toward the weapon. Confidently he kicked the gun aside. Yoshima then moved toward Carver. He assumed the position of Choy Li Fut, a murderous alliance of karate and Western combat. His hands were angled and rigid.

Carver relaxed, his hands at chest level. Fingers stiff, ready to strike. Yoshima moved warily, then whipped a hand out, feinted, and whirled on one foot. Carver easily avoided the shoe that slashed inches from his jaw.

A blaze of lightning lit up the ship.

Yoshima jerked at the brilliant light. Carver struck Yoshima in the midriff. Followed with a combination of chops and jabs. Yoshima staggered back; he bared his teeth and his hands trembled. He went into the Praying Mantis position, rocking on the balls of his feet.

Carver moved fast—feinted. Yoshima moved like liquid to counterstrike. The blow never landed. Carver's feint was a strike across Yoshima's face. Blood spurted from Yoshima's nose. Carver spun and hit the man across the chest.

Yoshima staggered back. He gasped for breath. He slipped on the deck and went down. He tried to rise. Carver stepped in and punched him with his fist. Yoshima rocked back on his heels. Carver punched him twice more. Harold Yoshima sprawled to the deck.

Rain beat down on his unconscious face.

A roll of thunder rolled through the storm.

Carver dragged him through the door into the corridor. He opened cabin doors until he found the cabin Yoshima shared with an officer. He found a thin towel in the washroom. He tore it into strips and bound and gagged Yoshima.

There were more yells from the bridge. The ship trembled as the engines turned over.

Carver went outside and got his overcoat and hat. He recovered the Colt Python. He returned to Yoshima's cabin. He flipped open the lids of luggage. In a small bag he found the dummy mock-up of the poetry anthology.

On the tenth page he noticed a period somewhat larger than others. He scraped at it with a fingernail. Yeah. It was some three-dimensional object. Holding it close, he studied it. A microdot.

He flipped through other pages. He found several dots. Undoubtedly there were many microdots scattered throughout.

He wrestled Yoshima over his shoulders in a fireman's carry. He stepped into the corridor.

The Japanese officer from the salon waited. He held a Nambu pistol on Carver.

"Interpol," Carver said, and gave the officer a brief glimpse of his ID wallet.

The officer shook his head.

"No, sir," he said in excellent English, "you are not from the international police. I know of you. The black confidential investigator. You have no jurisdiction on board without the proper legal documents. Please—put down Mr. Yoshima."

The man over Carver's shoulder wriggled.

"No," Carver said. "He's stolen important documents." He held out the bag with the mock-up papers.

"That may be so, but the laws of your country would decide such a matter. Is this not so? In the meantime, we must sail. We shall move from the dock in just a few minutes. Put Mr. Yoshima down.''

The officer raised his arm. He aimed between Carver's eyes.

THIRTY-FOUR

They stood there for a long moment. The ship's horn blew. The *Shika Maru* trembled.

Carver saw the officer's finger tighten on the trigger.

"Okay," Carver said, and dumped Harold Yoshima to the floor.

Yoshima jerked himself into a sitting position.

The steel door opened, and a gust of wind and rain swept into the corridor. A man stepped over the sill. And fired a shot at the officer.

The bullet whined off the metal wall.

"Drop it," Jack Bovee said.

The officer lowered his pistol. Bovee warned him a second time, and he let the pistol fall.

"I thought—" Carver started.

"I got washed between the pilings," Bovee explained, and gestured to the Japanese officer to move back. "Then I climbed out. Fixed myself up in the old apartment. I went back—and I was lucky. I followed you and that cop. I played it out like you'd figure where Yoshima would be." He gestured with the pistol at the man on the floor. "I was right. I was right behind you, all the way to the East Wind plant—and then here. Yeah, bro', you're smart.''

Bovee told Carver to tear off Yoshima's gag. Carver did it.

"Jack, Jack," Yoshima said with relief, "you're terrific. What a friend." On the floor, he rubbed at his feet and hands. "Come on! Let's get Bascombe—"

"Fuck Bascombe. And fuck you, too, Yosh. Don't get up. Stay down, you shit! You shot me.''

"What? Me? Jack, no—I swear, Jack, I never shot at you. It was an accident! I was trying to shoot—"

"Bullshit. My shoulder hurts like hell, but it's worth it. Don't get up, Yosh, don't even twitch. You were going to take all the money for yourself!" He turned to Carver. "Get off the boat. I'll be right behind you.''

"No," Carver said.

"I got no shit against you, bro', but you gotta get the fuck off this boat. They're gettin' ready to cast off. I'll follow you off.''

"No—I've got to bring Yoshima in.''

Bovee shook his head. He shot Yoshima in the chest.

Yoshima fell back. He made gurgling sounds. He clutched feebly at his chest.

The Japanese officer gaped.

"Oh, Jesus," Yoshima said, and stared wide-eyed at Bovee. "Oh, God, Jack, God—''

Bovee shot Yoshima in the face. Bits of bone and blood spattered the Japanese officer's white pants. Bovee looked at Carver.

"Now—there's no reason to stay.''

He went to the steel door and threw it open. He gestured angrily with his gun and Carver stepped into the storm. Thunder boomed. They hurried across the deck. The gangplank shook under their feet. Jack Bovee and Carver Bascombe stepped down onto the wharf.

THIRTY-FIVE

Sergeant Ludlow and Lieutenant De Anza took hold of Jack Bovee.

"What happened, Carver?" De Anza shouted over the wind.

"Where's Yoshima, Bascombe?" Ludlow demanded loudly.

"He's on board," Carver yelled, and handed to De Anza the attaché case. "Here's the microchip designs."

"You let him get away?" Ludlow said.

Carver shrugged. Jack Bovee turned to Ludlow.

"I killed him."

"Hey, wait," Ludlow yelped. "You can't say that! I've got to read you your rights."

"Fuck the rights," Bovee said. "I shot and killed Harold Yoshima."

Ludlow read him his rights and led the poet off to a police car.

"Hot, hot," Rose Weinbaum said, and blew on the checks in her hands. "I love Frank Needlemeier. And Gordon Dale is a sweetie." She turned to Laura De Anza. "Even your check is okay."

"It's only the first payment," Laura De Anza said.

"Rose, you're a greedy person," Royal Blue added, her

197

voice without malice. She smiled at Carver, taking the sting from her remark.

Rose grinned, put the checks in her drawer, and lit a cigarette.

Several days had passed since Bovee was arrested. They were seated in the front room of the Victorian house. A Mendelssohn piece played quietly through the stereo. A log fire crackled in the fireplace. Shadows flickered on the walls.

Laura De Anza held Carver's arm. She had thanked him and hugged him. He had said little. One regret that ate at him was Mr. Netsuke's needless death; just one more crazed chip in Yoshima's mind and scheme. He did not voice his troubled thoughts.

Carver went to Royal and encircled her with his arms. They looked into each other's eyes. He quoted in a near whisper:

> *"Touches there*
> *spasms stretched through time*
> *delicious tremors of body chaos*
> *echoes of voices alone*
> *kissed there*
> *a multitude of pain and joy—"*

"You're such a romantic beast," Royal said, and snuggled close to him. "You know—I think I've got you figured out."

"Yeah?"

"Oh, don't get your hackles up. I meant—you're sort of a throwback—maybe to some long-ago age of chivalry."

"Don't put that on paper," Carver said. "You'd lose your readers' respect."

"What? All six hundred and twenty-three of them."

He held her close and kissed her.

"Don't sell yourself short."

"Carver, you have your own way of doing things. Deep inside you're really an old-fashioned romantic. You really like to help people."

In the inner recesses where Subconscious sleeps, where Ego lords, where Esteem preens, there was a chuckle. The hunting animal had sheathed its claws, put away its weapons, and rolled over laughing softly with satisfaction.

Carver Bascombe walked Royal Blue to the windows. Outside, several shafts of ghostly sunlight slanted out of the dark clouds. The air was calm, the trees were still, and the wet streets sparkled. The rain had stopped. The storm had passed.

Calm sea and prosperous voyage.

About the Author

Kenn Davis is an artist as well as a writer. The other volumes in the Carver Bascombe series of mysteries published by Fawcett are WORDS CAN KILL, MELTING POINT, NIJINSKY IS DEAD, AS OCTOBER DIES, and ACTS OF HOMICIDE.

Davis and his wife Elizabeth live in California.